24 Hours
The Trade

ANNETTE OPPENLANDER

First published by Annette Oppenlander, 2023
Averesch 93, 48683 Ahaus
First Edition
Visit the author's website at www.annetteoppenlander.com
Text copyright: Annette Oppenlander 2023
ISBN: 978-3-948100-49-0 eBook
ISBN: 978-3-948100-50-6 Paperback
Editing: Jennifer Kay Davies, The History Quill
Design: http://www.fiverr.com/akira007
© 2023 Annette Oppenlander

Also from Annette Oppenlander

English

A Different Truth *(historical mystery – boarding school Vietnam War Era)*
Escape from the Past: The Duke's Wrath I *(time-travel/gaming adventure trilogy)*
Escape from the Past: The Kid II
Escape from the Past: At Witches' End III
Surviving the Fatherland: A True Coming-of-age Love Story Set in WWII
(biographical – WWII and postwar)
47 Days *(biographical novella – WWII)*
Everything We Lose: A Civil War Novel of Hope, Courage and Redemption
Where the Night Never Ends: A Prohibition Era Novel
When They Made Us Leave *(WWII young adult)*
Boys No More *(WWII – collection)*
A Lightness in My Soul *(biographical novella – WWII)*
The Scent of a Storm *(WWII and German Reunification)*
So Close to Heaven *(biographical – Napoleon Wars)*
When the Skies Rained Freedom *(Berlin Airlift)*

German

Vaterland, wo bist Du? Roman nach einer wahren Geschichte
(2. Weltkrieg/Nachkriegszeit – biografisch)
Erzwungene Wege: Historischer Roman *(2. Weltkrieg – Kinderlandverschickung)*
47 Tage: Wie zwei Jungen Hitlers letztem Befehl trotzten *(2. Weltkrieg – biografische Novelle)*
Erfolgreich(e) historische Romane schreiben *(Sachbuch)*
Immer der Fremdling: Die Rache des Grafen *(Mittelalter – Gaming Zeitreise)*
Als Deutschlands Jungen ihre Jugend verloren *(2. Weltkrieg – Sammlung)*
Bis uns nichts mehr bleibt *(amerikanischer Bürgerkrieg – Abenteuerroman)*
Ewig währt der Sturm *(2. Weltkrieg – Flucht und Vertreibung)*
Leicht wie meine Seele *(2. Weltkrieg – biografische Novelle)*

Endlos ist die Nacht (*amerikanische Prohibition – Abenteuerroman*)
Das Kreuz des Himmels (*Napoleon Kriege – biografisch*)
Zwei Handvoll Freiheit *(Nachkriegszeit/ Berliner Luftbrücke –*
historischer Liebesroman)
24 Stunden: Tauschgeschäfte (*2. Weltkrieg – biografische Novelle*)

DEDICATION

For my father, Günter, whose grit and determination continue to amaze me.

"If you win, you need not have to explain… If you lose, you should not be there to explain!" —Adolf Hitler

"Through clever and constant application of propaganda, people can be made to see paradise as hell, and also the other way round, to consider the most wretched sort of life as paradise." —Adolf Hitler

hun·ger / ˈhəNGgər/ *a feeling of discomfort or weakness caused by lack of food, coupled with the desire to eat, a weakened condition brought about by prolonged lack of food.*

In Loving Memory...

Günter
Schmidt

12/20/1928 - 09/21/2021

TUESDAY, DECEMBER 19, 1944

EIGHT O'CLOCK

I awoke from Mother's knocking. Why couldn't she let me sleep? At least when I slept, I forgot about life for a bit. My gaze wandered to the empty bed across from me. My brother, Hans, had been gone for nearly three months. Just yesterday, we'd received a postcard with a scribbled note that he was stationed across the Rhine, less than forty miles from here. None of his cards said much, as if he were in too much of a hurry. The truth was that he wasn't allowed to write things. Like Father, who'd been gone for four and a half years, the field post of soldiers was censured. Not just to hide any news of the war, but because the government intended to hide the real state of the country.

As if that was necessary, as if we didn't realize how bad things were. Everything was rationed... Food, clothes, shoes, coal, and every month those rations grew smaller. You couldn't buy sewing needles, paper, pens or light bulbs. They just didn't exist anymore. Of course, since the city had been bombed six weeks ago, we had no electricity anyway. Nor running water. Life was a disaster from start to finish.

I sighed, the noise strange in the stillness, along with my steaming breath. Our apartment was freezing cold and gloomy, thanks to the boarded-up window, a patchwork of linoleum, tarpaper and wood scraps—my handiwork. The bombing had also destroyed every piece of glass or mirror and for a week afterwards,

I'd hammered together whatever I could find to keep the icy winter air at bay.

"Are you up?" Mother's voice crept through the closed door. "I could use some help."

"Coming." Reluctantly, I crept out of bed, pulling on the one outfit that still fit somewhat. My big toe stuck through the tip of the sock Mother had already darned three times. Already, I dreaded the walk to the public water hole where we fetched drinking water. It was a ten-minute walk, fifteen with full buckets. But it was one thing to carry water to drink or cook with, another entirely to fill a tub for a bath.

Not only did I have to go three times, but a good portion of that water also had to be heated. And firewood was another issue. Usually, Helmut, my best friend, and I went into the woods to cut trees down—which was forbidden, or we searched bombsites, which was also forbidden. Beneath the rubble was plenty of torn-apart wood... Floorboards, pieces of furniture, roof trusses. But each piece had to be cut and carried home. My little brother, Siegfried, was only eight and no help. And Mother?

Another sigh rose into the air. Mother had enough on her plate to keep us going. First, she'd seen Father being drafted into this endless war, then Hans. I knew she worried about me going as well. When she felt unobserved, she paced around the room or patted the stack of field post, tied with a blue ribbon. It was the only piece of color that remained in the house, a fragile piece of fabric that could fall apart at any moment.

Pulling on my sweater, I entered the kitchen, where Mother was washing dishes in a zinc bowl and Siegfried was awkwardly drying them.

My gaze immediately wandered to the table where 'breakfast' was waiting for me. What a joke. I sat down, eyeing the piece of cornbread, thinly scraped with something red, passing itself off as strawberry jam. As a reminder, my stomach rumbled.

"I wanted to make tea," Mother said, drying her hands. "But firewood is low, and I was going to save it for dinner."

"I'll grab some this morning," I said, taking a careful bite of the bread. It tasted bland, because we had no salt, and the red goo scraped on top had no flavor at all.

Mother slumped on the chair across from me. "You also need to pick up rations." She pushed several coupon cards across the table. Bread, it said on one, meat and eggs on others. "Supposedly, we're getting sugar this week."

I stuffed the cards into my pant pocket, keeping my thoughts to myself. Every week they told us what food we were going to receive and how much. Most of the time, the store shelves were long empty when I got there and the allotments we did receive were much smaller than announced.

The last bite of bread disappeared. To chase away the rumbles, I downed a cup of water, then another.

Mother's small hand landed on mine. "I'm sorry, Günter. I wish you'd not have to work all the time. I wish we had more to eat." She fidgeted and tugged at her hair she wore in a loose knot. Women no longer visited the hairdresser because a while back, it had been forbidden—most hairdressers had long been drafted anyway.

When had those creases appeared on her forehead? When had she stopped smiling? I couldn't remember, couldn't remember the last time we'd all sat at a dinner table together as a family, or the last time I'd eaten a full meal.

I pushed away the anger that accompanied me through most days. It wasn't Mother's fault that we starved. Or that Father and Hans fought some place for a man who was insane. Nobody said it aloud, but we all knew that the war was lost and that it was just a matter of time before…

Before what? Would we starve to death, or would I be called to serve, too? Maybe the bombs would do their job next time and finish us all. And to think that tomorrow was my sixteenth birthday. What a joke. Not that I cared for any gifts, but how I longed for a little celebration… A candle, a piece of apple pie.

Rising abruptly, I said, "I'll get firewood first."

Mother followed me to the door and touched my cheek. "Be careful."

3

NINE O'CLOCK—MORNING

I was already tired before I began. And cold. Being hungry did something to the body, something that surprised me every time. It robbed my breath, took my energy to the point that I was shivering. A general feeling of weakness crept into my legs, and starting at the ankles it crawled higher, to my knees and into my thighs until I moved like that war vet living next door, the one with the crutches and the grayish skin.

Father's voice resounded in my head. *Work yourself warm*, he'd said, trying for a smile.

He'd returned for a visit five weeks ago. They called it *Bombenurlaub*—'bomb vacation.' When a soldier's family at home had suffered bomb attacks, soldiers were allowed to leave their troops to visit and inspect what was left.

Laughable, right? Father had received Category B, which meant that living quarters needed substantial work, but family members were healthy. For fourteen days, he'd helped us repair the apartment house, had climbed onto the roof with me, because the other neighbors were too old or feeble to collect and reinstall what was left of the clay shingles and patch up holes with tarpaper. We'd picked up firewood and sorted through broken china, swept up the remains of flour and sugar. There was only one thing Father had been unable to do: fill our cupboards and our stomachs. He'd been appalled at our rations, and ultimately helpless.

Yet, for those fourteen days I'd allowed myself to dream of him being home... Staying home. Like a family. Like we used to be.

4

Inevitably, the day had come when he'd left once more. Somewhere to the Balkans, he'd said when we hugged. Mother had cried, Siegfried too. Only I had kept it together, swallowing and breathing through my nose. The tears came later when I was lying alone in my bed.

In a way, I resented his visit. For a while, I'd gone through the motions without him, kind of gotten used to things. But now, with the memory of him here with us fresh in my mind, the difference had become clear. Missing him hurt like a fresh wound. The scab had been removed; new blood was flowing.

I trudged to Brühler Straße, where several houses had been reduced to rubble. To my left towered the four-story bunker, completed two years ago, where Mother and Siegfried hid whenever the air raid sirens warned of approaching enemy planes. I never went with them, not since that one day when I'd come along and found out that I couldn't stand being locked in.

Invisible hands had choked me to the point I thought I'd pass out. Now, I just glared at the monstrous building with the narrow slots for windows. The walls had to be six feet thick and reminded me of a giant stone grave. To bring in enough oxygen, the people inside had to turn the crank of a fan. It still wasn't enough, the air thick as soup. After a few minutes it became difficult to form a thought, and all I wanted to do was lie down and never get up again.

To my right, the remnants of several former houses rose to a mountain of rubble. A couple of women, hair wrapped in scarves, hands wrapped with strips of fabric, were picking up bricks in search of treasure, maybe a pot or some silverware, something that could be used or traded.

I crept to the edges in the back, where a former garden shed had been crushed and buried. Glass splinters sparkled in the sunlight, strangely beautiful among the wreckage. I pulled out a piece of framing, a precarious task because at any second the ground could shift, making me lose my balance, slide into a hole or get stuck. Already the skin on my palms ached from the rough edges. I needed Helmut to help. He lived up the street, not more than a five-minute walk from here, yet I couldn't make myself go up there. It took energy to stop and climb down, energy I didn't have.

My stomach rumbled once more, reminding me that the slice of bread this morning had long since been digested. I took a deep breath and sat down, letting the wave of dizziness pass that often accompanied the hunger pangs. I inspected my hands, the skin on my fingers dusty and chafed. To chase away the stiffness from the cold, I blew into them.

Nothing got accomplished sitting here, so I rose once more to continue. The pile of wood grew, though some pieces were too large to carry. I had brought Father's saw and began to cut a beam into two three-foot pieces. I'd have to cut them again in order to fit them into the oven, but for now that could wait.

At last, I wrapped them with a piece of cord I always carried for such tasks. The pack was heavy, almost too heavy to manage, especially across the rubble. I bent forward, set my feet carefully to keep my balance.

After a hundred yards, I rested again. The ache in my back had joined the ache in my belly. How much longer could I work like this on almost nothing to eat? My body was protesting, telling me to either feed it or quit moving so much. I could do neither. I had to endure. Somehow.

ELEVEN O'CLOCK—MORNING

Mother watched me stash the wood in the corner of the kitchen. We couldn't risk putting it in the basement because now that the front door no longer closed—it'd been torn from its hinges during the bombing and only provisionally repaired—people could sneak inside to search for things to steal. Everyone did it, I couldn't even fault them, but nothing down in the cellars where we'd kept our tools was safe now.

I washed my hands and downed the last of the drinking water. That was my next job.

"Siegfried and I could come along," Mother said, watching me from the bench where she darned my sock.

I wiped my hands on the towel that doubled as a drying cloth and shook my head. "I'll take care of it. Besides, we only have two buckets. I might as well carry them both."

"I could cut the firewood." Siegfried took hold of the axe I'd placed next to the stove. He was small for his age, skinny like me with the brown eyes of my mother. Born eight years after me, he'd been a 'surprise' for my parents.

I gently took the axe from his hands and said, "Better let me take care of that."

Siegfried made a face. "I want to help."

"You can help me clean the kitchen, once Günter brings the water," Mother said.

Siegfried climbed back on the kitchen chair, where he'd been reading one of my old books, *Lampe's Weekend, a Funny Hare*

Excursion. "Boring."

"How about you accompany me to the well?"

Mother and I exchanged a glance. I knew she was fiercely protective of her youngest and there was always a chance of another air raid. In the early days of the war, most bombers had come at night, sneaking up on the cities to drop their bombs while remaining undetected. These days the bombers flew too high to be fended off by the anti-aircraft cannons or *Flaks*—if there were even any left— so they attacked any time of day or night.

But I refused to be afraid, refused to let them dictate my day and occupy my thoughts. It was bad enough to constantly think about organizing provisions and wood. "It'll be fine," I said.

Siegfried had jumped back down and wiggled from one foot to another. "Please, Mother, let me go with Günter."

I knew I'd be even slower with my little brother, but at least he distracted me from my own misery. I'd noticed that Mother was sharing some of her own rations with him, so he was doing better than me. Still, I didn't mind. He was small enough and kids died all the time from dysentery or hunger typhus. Both were caused by lack of hygiene which explained why Mother insisted on washing our clothes and beds and scrubbing each room every week no matter how hard it was.

I let Siegfried carry one of the empty buckets for a while, until he grew tired.

"You think Father will come back soon?" he asked, his dark eyes on me. "Mother doesn't want to talk about it." We had left the bunker behind us and were walking up Wachtelstraße.

"I hope so. He thinks the war will end soon."

"How soon?"

That was the million-dollar question. There was no telling. Even if the newspaper, now reduced to a couple of pages, showed columns of obituaries of fallen soldiers, even if more and more cities lay in ruin, Hitler was not bowing down. Just the opposite; the paper spoke of heroic battles and great conquests—the *Endsieg*... 'the final victory'. How could we be victorious when the city lay in ruin, when thousands of civilians had died and twenty thousand had lost the roofs over their heads in Solingen alone?

When Hans had left in October, Mother had mumbled how the Führer was intent on murdering everyone. In a moment when she'd thought to be unobserved, she'd said it to herself, a comment that could kill if it were overheard by the wrong people. I knew she was angry about the government, angry that Hitler was willing to sacrifice the entire nation. He'd even said it himself. If Germany couldn't win, there was no point in having a Germany. He likely squatted in some bunker in Berlin while Father and Hans were risking their necks.

"…soon?"

"What?" I'd completely forgotten that Siegfried was walking next to me.

"I asked how soon Father will return home."

"Hard to say. Though I can't imagine that the war will continue much longer."

Siegfried looked thoughtful. How could he comprehend the disastrous life we were leading? And yet, he seemed quite wise. After all, he'd known nothing but war. Since as soon as he was old enough to remember, the war had been going on. "I hope Hans is safe."

Hearing those words from my little brother's lips let the tears that sometimes pressed come dangerously close. I cleared my throat and forced a chuckle. "He'll be fine. You know him, he's always smart."

But smart had little to do with surviving as a soldier. Often it was a matter of luck where you were stationed. As a soldier you had no say; you had to obey orders from some fellow who was told by his superior. And we all knew who that was.

A line of ragged-looking people was waiting in front of the well, housed within a small stone building from which the water gushed into a terracotta-colored stone trough. The entire neighborhood, hundreds of people, came here every day to fetch water because the water utility company had also been bombed seven weeks ago.

Waiting lines were great harbingers of news: stories passed from mouth to mouth, then were carried home afterwards. Things like a delivery of bread at a particular store or where you could cut trees unobserved, who had died or was rumored to be in a prison camp—news from the front, trickling in by field post. Most of all, people whispered about the missing. Not only those who'd disappeared during the bombings in Solingen and across the country, but husbands, brothers, uncles and sons who'd not written from the front in months and whose fate was unknown.

Like my father's. Even if he'd been home not long ago, there was no guarantee he'd return. Any moment could take him away permanently.

When Siegfried pulled my sleeve—he'd visited a classmate back in the line—I was surprised that we were already at the front of the line. *Stop daydreaming and concentrate*, my mind commented. *You need your wits about you.* The water ran fast and cold from the spigot, filled our buckets in seconds.

"Let me carry one," Siegfried said.

"It's all right, two are easier to carry than one." It was true; and besides, in Siegfried's hands, the water would slosh out, leaving us with half the amount. "Why don't you tell me about your friend?"

TWELVE O'CLOCK—NOON

Against my better judgment, I'd hoped for a decent lunch, but all we sat down to when we returned home was another slice of cornbread, this time scraped with something called margarine. It had nothing in common with the margarine or butter before the war, tasted more like mineral oil scraped from the bottom of a car engine.

Still, I was thankful to chew and swallow. It is challenging to pace yourself when you're hungry. Your instinct says to wolf down everything in record speed, but from experience you know it is better and at least in your mind more satisfying to eat slowly. Every meal was a struggle; during every meal my mind was fighting my needy body. At least Mother had made peppermint tea which warmed me on the inside and added a feeling of fullness.

"I spoke with Frau Sanders," Mother said, watching us eat. Supposedly, she'd already had lunch which I doubted. I'd overheard Father talk to her and voice his concern about her thinness. She was kind of short anyway and likely didn't weigh more than a hundred pounds.

"You need your strength, Grete," Father had whispered. "Think of the boys."

"That's what I'm doing," she'd said just as quietly.

Father had clucked and shaken his head, but as soon as he'd become aware of my presence, he'd changed the subject.

"She says our grocery store is closed. I hope it isn't true."

"I'll pick up rations as soon as I'm done here." I was only half listening, because I was inspecting the wooden beams that still demanded to be cut.

"I think you better go right away. We may have to find another store. Who knows how long the lines will be." It was true. Lines were everywhere these days... At the stores, the well, the ration office where we picked up cards, the coal trader and the kiosk to get a precious newspaper. Most of the time the waiting was fruitless, and the items we'd waited in line for were gone by the time it was our turn.

On the way out the door, I thought longingly of the sofa where I used to sit quietly and read. These days there was hardly any time for such pleasure.

I'd thought that when the schools closed, I'd have plenty of time to run around and hang out with Helmut. But we always had to help our families, run errands, or do chores.

ONE O'CLOCK—AFTERNOON

The wind had picked up when I re-entered the street. Afternoon clouds hung low, tingeing the air gray and threatening rain. Hugging myself, I hurried along the footpath that had formed across the rubble. On Zweigstraße, a number of homes had collapsed and burned, the rocks blackened and emitting a faint smell of phosphor and soot. The Royal Air Force loved to throw two different types of bombs. The first was a heavy pointy thing that crashed through the roofs of houses all the way to the basement. Then in a second run, they'd follow up with phosphor bombs that burned so hot, it sucked the oxygen from the air around. Those lucky enough to escape the fire suffocated because of it.

Ignoring the stench, I hurried on. Places like these held no wood nor anything else useful. Like hungry wolves, the superheated fires had taken it all. I gazed at the sky, wondering if more bombers would come. Likely yes. As long as the war continued, they'd drop their deadly loads.

Why couldn't that idiot in Berlin see that it was over and put a stop to it? Why did he let us suffer, allow people to die, not just the soldiers, but the kids and mothers who were staying home?

A sigh escaped me, rose like a cry into the air. Nobody cared; the world had turned against us because we'd started a horrific war, attacked more than thirty countries, killed millions. Now it was time for us to suffer.

I didn't notice the sign until I tried opening the door: *Closed until further notice*. No explanation, no reopening date. Frau Sanders had been right.

What was I supposed to do now? The prospect of going home to a handful of shriveled potatoes for dinner made me slow... then stop. I couldn't return home. Not like this.

"Günter, wait," Helmut shouted, running toward me. "Are you picking up food?"

He came to a stop, panting. Five inches taller than me, he looked gaunt, his eyes shiny and large, his nose seemingly too large for his face. Despite the starvation rations, he'd grown during the summer, revealing bony ankles beneath pants held up by lengths of twine.

"They're closed." I couldn't keep the despair from my voice. "You want to try another store?"

To my surprise Helmut's eyes sparkled with excitement. "Maybe later. I just heard about an army convoy heading through town. Maybe our dads are with them." Helmut lowered his voice. "Our neighbor says the Wehrmacht is retreating."

Hitler wouldn't allow a retreat. At least not officially.

Against my will, I imagined myself in a tight embrace with my father. Since he'd left, we'd heard nothing, if he'd arrived safely or how his return trip had been. Not that that was unusual. Sometimes many months went by without a sign of life. Then two cards would arrive in a span of a week. Mail was another thing that no longer worked reliably.

The worry of losing him in one of the terrible battles returned. Men simply disappeared, while families waited for news, waited— for a letter, a card or the hero's note of condolence from Hitler's regime. Especially if they had been in battles in the east—like my father was now.

"He won't be there." I shook my head to discourage my own hope. Thinking of the ration cards in my pocket and the paltry dinner that would turn out even skimpier than usual, I added, "We've got to check another store."

"But maybe they've got news." Helmut wiggled from one foot to the other. His dad hadn't come home for bomb vacation, and I knew he was worried all the time. How could I deny my best friend a chance to see his father?

"All right."

Helmut grinned. "Let's hurry, we don't want to miss them."

On Neuenhoferstraße, we turned left, away from downtown and the total destruction there. We knew every road here, every path and every house, most of them small, sided with shale shingles like dull gray fish scales. This was *our* neighborhood, Höhscheid, a place where blue-collar workers, dye makers, metal and sword smiths, and polishers worked and lived in Solingen's steel ware industry. Most were gone now, having replaced their leather aprons and cutting tools with guns or relocated to some weapons factory.

The closer we came to the edge of town, where the road leads downhill and out of town, the more people we noticed. Women and children lined the sidewalks and peered anxiously down the street. Instead of looking at the Rhine River valley in the distance, they fixated on the men snaking uphill in an endless procession. The soldiers' eyes were downcast in faces expressionless and hidden under a coat of grime, their movements as mechanical as rusty machines, their boots filthy and their uniforms stained and torn. I scanned the faces, one by one, until my eyes blurred. Nobody looked familiar, not even a neighbor. Farther down the hill, a man was leading a horse.

"These men aren't from here," I said as we walked past the cheering women and children. Why they cheered, I didn't know. Maybe to make the men feel better or maybe because it made them feel like they were doing something useful. But no matter how I stared, the faces were unfamiliar. Father was not among them, nor was Helmut's. "We should go. I doubt they can tell us anything."

Helmut ignored me. "Is he waving at us? Look."

I reluctantly turned and stared at the approaching men. Indeed, the soldier with the horse seemed to point in our direction, though he could mean anybody standing nearby. Likely he'd discovered his wife among the spectators.

When the soldier was thirty yards away, he broke away from his troop and headed our way. Around us, nobody cried or waved, so I punched Helmut in the side. "Let's go meet him."

TWO O'CLOCK—AFTERNOON

The closer we drew, the more haggard and sickly the man looked, his eyes glassy, rimmed red from infection or lack of sleep. His mare had seen better days, too. Angular hip bones protruded from the animal's shanks held together by rugged brown skin. Sores festered where the saddle had been, a caricature of a once proud warhorse.

The soldier waved. "Boys, come here—quickly."

We hurried near as he kept looking back at his troop. What was wrong with him? Helmut seemed to have no reservations and rushed to meet the man, so I followed.

The horse man's gaze flitted back to the men marching uphill not twenty yards behind him, then back to us. He lowered his head and whispered, "I need civilian clothes and shoes. Any chance you can spare some?"

I wrinkled my nose as the stench from weeks of unwashed skin crawled up my nostrils. Dirt coated the man's neck and the grayish chin covered with stubble. I thought of Mother always scrubbing our clothes and insisting on baths, no matter how hard it was to fill the zinc tub. This man surely had lice; maybe he had that terrible dysentery. He sure reeked like an outhouse.

Helmut and I looked at each other. What were we supposed to say? Clothes weren't exactly growing on trees these days, especially winter jackets and sturdy shoes.

Behind him the convoy kept marching; creeping was more like it. Again, the soldier peeked over his shoulder, then back at us. He seemed relaxed, but I sensed his nervousness, a fear like that of an animal trapped in a cage.

Somewhere downhill, an engine revved. The horse man's chin began to tremble as he patted the horse's neck.

The sound of an engine grew louder and a VW *Kübelwagen*, a car reminding me of a bucket on wheels, appeared, an officer visible in the backseat. Brass buttons gleamed like foreign objects in the afternoon light.

"I'll give you my horse," the soldier mumbled with a quivering voice. "She used to be a fine mare." He glanced at the poor creature standing behind him with a hanging head. "They tell us not to get attached." He shrugged. "I guess I can't help myself. She's been with me for five years." Sadness crept into his voice as he rubbed a grimy sleeve over his eyes.

I felt a strange curiosity, but also pity. The man had fought for years, struggled to survive in this madness just like Father. He wanted out like we all did. And he was obviously afraid. After what we'd heard about deserters or people speaking up against the regime, it was no surprise. They even hung posters in shop windows, warning men to desert. Helping a deserter was just as dangerous.

"Sure, I've got clothes," I heard myself say, feeling Helmut's gaze on my temple.

"Shhh." The man casually flicked a chunk of mud from the horse's flank because by now the VW was only fifteen yards away. The man in the back was eying us, as if he wanted to extract the truth from our brains.

"From my father," I hurried under my breath. "He's in the war, too. Any chance you know him? Artur… Schmidt?"

The man grimaced and shook his head.

"Sorry, son, I don't know your father. There're too many of us." After another glimpse at the approaching car, he continued. "Where do you live?"

Helmut was tugging at my sleeve, but I shook him off. I'd go door to door to find clothes to trade. "Not far, maybe a kilometer or two. Can you come with us?"

"No!" The man sounded afraid again. "I have to stay with my company. We must meet after dark." Behind the man, the car's engine roared.

My knees trembled, but this was the break I'd hoped for. We could do a lot with this horse. "We'll follow you to town," I said under my breath. "On the way we'll watch for a meeting spot."

"Everything all right here?" The well-dressed officer straightened inside the open VW and suspiciously eyed the soldier… and me.

"*Jawohl, Herr Hauptmann*," the soldier yelled, throwing up an arm with the Hitler greeting.

"Sir, he… I asked him about my father?" I said. Why didn't I shut up? "He is in the war, too. Maybe you know him. His name is Artur Schm—"

"Not much chance of that." The officer impatiently shouted at his driver. As the horse soldier hurried off without another look, I felt my knees go soft. "Say, you." The officer's voice cut like glass shards.

I froze and turned toward the car. The buttons on the man's coat gleamed like gold, surreal in the grayness of the afternoon, the wasteland of my hometown. "Yes, sir?"

"Shouldn't you be serving by now? How old are you?"

"I'll be sixteen tomorrow. They haven't called me yet." Despite the December wind, sweat dripped under my shirt. The man's eyes were light blue, sort of watery, and yet I sensed the fanaticism that propelled him forward, made him shout at the hovel of downtrodden men. I wanted to slap him, tell him to shut up and tell his boss to leave us be. Of course, I did no such thing. Mouthing off to an officer could land me in trouble, maybe get me shot or taken to the front which was as good as being dead.

"You'll get your chance to serve our *Führer* soon." The officer whipped an arm across the windshield. "*Heil* Hitler."

I raised my arm, but the man had already ordered his driver to take off. He revved the engine, and the VW left us in a cloud of exhaust fumes.

"That was close." Helmut's face was pale as flour.

I let out a breath. No time to be afraid. "Do you see the man with the horse?" Uphill, soldiers and trucks disappeared in a dust cloud.

"What are you thinking?" Helmut asked as he followed my gaze.

"Catch up to the horse soldier, find a place to meet later."

Helmut huffed. "You aren't serious. Did you not see that officer? He'd shoot you on the spot if he knew. That horse man, too."

"I'm going to trade that horse." In my mind I already saw myself hand a pile of neatly packaged meat to my mother.

"Are you nuts?" Helmut's voice was shrill. "Where will you get clothes anyway?"

I walked faster. "I'll think of something." I produced a smile even if my insides felt weak with hunger and worry. The old rumble was back, spreading its tentacles to my brain. A thousand things could go wrong. "Keep an eye out for the car," I whispered as Helmut hurried alongside. Along the road, women and children continued to cheer the passing soldiers; some watched silently.

"What are you *doing?*"

"You heard him, he needs clothes and we'll get some."

"They'll shoot us," Helmut hissed. He looked ready to throw up.

I placed a forefinger across my lips and shook my head. There were people everywhere. Most were harmless, some were not. It was impossible to know.

THREE O'CLOCK—AFTERNOON

Ahead, the company had stopped and began settling under a stand of oak trees, which had survived among homes now reduced to ruins. We were still a hundred yards away when I noticed an old barn behind a deserted house, its roof a black, gaping hole.

I veered toward the barn, hoping that Helmut would follow. Despite my strong words, I knew we were taking a huge risk. But there was Mother waiting for her rations, rations I wasn't going to deliver. Siegfried, watching me as I swallowed a piece of bread.

"This should work," I mumbled, entering what was left of the barn. The dirt floor was bare, though it smelled faintly of straw and manure. Despite its missing roof, the walls held together surprisingly well—strange that nobody had cut away the wooden planks yet.

When we walked back outside, I understood why. To the left of the barn stood a two-story home that was mostly intact. The barn belonged to it.

Helmut pulled me to a stop, his face close to me. "What are you going to do? What if the officer sees you?"

I sucked in a mouthful of freezing air and straightened my back. Sometimes I wished Helmut would shut up. Not because he was wrong; just the opposite. "Wait here."

Afraid of losing confidence, I forced my shoulders to drop casually and wandered toward camp. Helmut was right, of course. This was insane. But then my stomach rumbled, a dull ache that accompanied me from morning till night. I was stinking tired of being hungry... and afraid.

My heart pounded in my throat as I eyed the VW parked near the main road. Likely, the officer was inside the man-high tent next to it.

Fifty feet away, the horse soldier was on his knees, rolling out a stained military blanket, his horse tethered to a tree stump. Next to him other men were settling in, some pitching low tents, others sorting through their packs. Two men were starting a cook fire; another was walking off with two buckets.

"Leave," the horse man said as I approached, sounding irritated and terrified at the same time.

Ignoring the man's annoyance, I fell to my knees and pretended to help straighten out his blanket, nodding casually at the old shack. "We can meet you over there."

"When?"

"Nine tonight?"

"Yes," the soldier breathed.

In the distance Helmut was trying to appear relaxed while leaning against the barn. "What size shoes do you wear?"

"Doesn't matter."

I slowly rose and, resisting the urge to run, strolled toward the barn, all the while expecting the officer shouting or somebody ramming a pistol into my back. Had anyone overheard our conversation? After all the stories of neighbors spying on neighbors, turning in friends and even family members to the SS, I was paranoid, my legs and feet weak as jelly.

Walk, my mind urged.

Helmut pulled me into the barn. He looked green. "You're crazy."

"Just hungry."

Helmut gave a tiny nod. How often had we scrounged around the area in search of something to chew? Half ripe apples, rutabagas, nettles, anything we could take home to our mothers for another meal. Now we had a real opportunity. I wasn't about to let it get away.

"What did he say?"

"We meet at nine here in the barn."

Helmut frowned, which made his beaky nose look even longer. "You promised him a bunch of clothes. I don't think we've got much left."

I thought about Mother's comments about the ever-increasing

collections for clothes. The winter relief showed up at our door all the time now, asking for donations of jackets and pants, of shoes and household goods to help returning veterans or orphaned children. As if we had much to give at this time. It felt like being squeezed so long, there was no juice left in the lemon. Pushing away the worry about finding something suitable for the horse man, I peeked over my shoulder. Somewhere in the fading light, I imagined the reflection of brass buttons.

"Let's go."

FOUR O'CLOCK—AFTERNOON

Helmut raced off as if a pack of wolves were after him. Only five days before Christmas Eve, dusk was already setting, but I took my time. I needed time to calm my nerves. We hadn't had any street lanterns for years, and every house was required to cover up any light sources. Not that we had much to show. Without electricity and hardly a candle around, the town sunk into blackness every night.

Luckily Helmut slowed down. It was never a good idea to run when you couldn't see much. Many sidewalks had disappeared; holes and bomb craters dotted the area. We picked our way down Platzhofstraße, then left into Weinsbergtal. Now that we'd left the excitement behind, I felt cold once more. The icy air seemed to crawl beneath my skin. After the horrible bombing and the subsequent fires, the entire city had been covered in dust. Dust from the rubble, ashes from the fires. Then came the rain. Six weeks of it. Not just drizzle, but hard-pouring torrents of rain that had turned the ground into sticky gunk, soiling my shoes and the once clean linoleum of my home.

"Let's go and see what we have," Helmut said when I caught up to him. "Man, I'm starving."

I didn't need any reminders and just grunted.

"Mother will be mad," he continued.

"About what?"

"That I want clothes." Helmut stopped to face me. "I mean, we don't even know if the man will still be there."

"Why wouldn't he?"

Helmut scratched his head, then stuck his hands back into his pockets. "What if he found someone else already? We may bust our butts for nothing."

In an instant I felt hot again. This time from anger. "I'm going to try, no matter what."

"I'm just saying—"

"I know what you're saying. You don't have to come," I bluffed. I couldn't imagine doing this on my own, but I was sick of our situation. Just the prospect of facing Mother without a shred of food was keeping me from going home.

Helmut sighed, a loud raspy sound in the stillness. "That's not what I mean, it's just…" He shrugged. "Oh, let's see what Mother has to say."

I followed my friend down the street, neither of us speaking until we reached the little half timber house in Unnersberg. The buildings here were at least a hundred years old with bowed walls and tiny rooms. Still, it didn't matter. At least Helmut still had a place to live.

"Mother," he called as soon as we entered.

"You're late." Holding a candle, Helmut's mother rushed toward us, crowding the tiny entry hall. "I was worried." Discovering me, she nodded with a tight smile. "Hello, Günter. How is your mother?"

"Fine, I think."

Helmut's mother eyed me carefully. "She's likely as worried as I am. Where have you boys been?" Her gaze traveled down to Helmut's hand where she surely expected to see a bag with rations. "No food? What happened?"

"I can explain." Helmut pulled me forward into the kitchen. "The store was locked up. I'm not sure what is going on, so we—"

"Why didn't you try somewhere else?" Helmut's mother slumped down at the table next to us. "We're just about out of everything."

I detected panic in her voice, something I knew from my own mother when things were getting tight. "We're going to trade a horse, *Frau Fuß*," I said, hoping to calm the tension.

"A horse?" Helmut's mother jumped back up, her arms swinging like the blades of a windmill. "What are we going to do with a horse?"

"Eat it, of course."

Helmut's mother slowly sank back onto her chair as a frown darkened her expression. "Somebody will just hand over a horse, which you will just butcher like a rabbit? What could we possibly have to trade?" she said, more to herself than to us.

"Civilian clothes," I blurted. "For a soldier."

"A deserter." Helmut's mother nodded. Then she jumped up again. "Are you out of your mind? What if they catch you?"

In the following stillness, Helmut's breath rattled loudly. "We'll be careful," he said finally. "I promise." He got up too, pulling his mother into an embrace. "We need your help, though."

"We need a jacket, pants, anything a man can wear."

Helmut's mother walked to the tiny window, then back, facing us again. "The only thing I can offer is a hat. The last collection from winter relief wiped us out."

I looked at Helmut whose expression reflected what I felt: defeat.

What if Mother had nothing left either? We had little time to ask other neighbors, and scrounging in the open was impossible in the dark.

Shaking off my frustration, I drained the peppermint tea Helmut's mother had made and headed home. By now my belly was roaring loudly and the heavy feeling from this morning was back. My legs felt as if I were carrying rocks in them as I crept through the dark streets.

I'd hoped that Helmut's mother had a pair of shoes or a sweater, but she'd even shown us her closet. Other than a handful of dresses for herself, there was nothing. And Helmut didn't own much more than what he was wearing. Somehow, tonight, I'd have to find enough to make this trade.

FIVE O'CLOCK—AFTERNOON

When I entered, Mother and Siegfried were sitting at the table, playing checkers.

"I'm home," I cried needlessly, anxious what they'd say about my news.

Mother jumped up, scanned my empty hands. "Where've you been? Where's our food?" Her gaze traveled to the counter where a lonely pot was sitting, undoubtedly waiting to be filled.

"Store's closed," I said, well aware that the news would make her even more anxious. "But I've got news—"

"What do you mean it's closed? What're we going to eat? Did you try a different place? Surely they can't all be—"

I caught Mother's flying hands like I'd calm a frightened baby bird. "Listen, I've got a real opportunity." Fresh excitement crept into my voice. "We met a man who'll give us his horse."

Mother stared at me while Siegfried crawled off the bench to take my hand. "Just like that?"

"He needs civilian clothes."

Mother swept a hand through her hair. "You can't be serious. He's a soldier defecting? You have any idea what happens if they catch you?"

"They won't."

But Mother wasn't done. "Civilian clothes. What is going on in this country?" She rounded back on me, hands on her hips. "What're you going to do with a military horse? If the SS gets wind of this…"

"It'll be dark. Nobody will see us." I placed a hand on Mother's shoulder. "Please. I need clothes. Can we check the closet?"

"He can have my old scarf," Siegfried cried, galloping out of the room and returning seconds later with a lumpy and matted scarf Mother was going to unravel and reuse for another project.

Meanwhile Mother began to pace. "Let's just say you're getting this horse."

I bit my lips, hiding my uncertainty. It was dangerous, but I was sick and tired of starving. "We'll find a way."

"Do you have any idea how hard it is to butcher? It's not a rabbit or chicken. You have to hide—"

"Helmut will help, we'll share the meat." I hugged my mother. "Don't worry." I quickly walked into the bathroom to hide my shaking hands. Clearing my throat, I called over my shoulder, "Better hurry."

When I emerged, Mother was waiting for me in the hallway. "Let's have a look." She led the way to her closet, opened it and began to rummage. "I've got very little left," she mumbled. "Your father will need a suit when he returns." A sigh escaped her. She wasn't saying it, but I knew how anxious she was about his absence and whether he'd ever wear a civilian suit again. Every morning she poured over the obituaries in the paper in search of names she recognized.

She pulled out a sweater, then a pair of pants Father used to wear in the garden. "It's not much, but it'll have to do."

"What about a jacket or coat?"

Mother didn't hear me and held up the sweater, sniffed.

"*Mutter*, please."

"It still smells a bit like him." Mother shook her head. "Maybe I'm imagining things." She handed over the sweater. "It'll keep the man warm."

"We need shoes, too."

My mother sighed again. "I only have one pair left—your father's best Sunday shoes." She pulled them off the bottom shelf and inspected the soles. "Like new," she mumbled, tucking the laces inside.

Hand them over, I wanted to shout. "I need a jacket," I said aloud.

"What if he never needs another pair?" Mother was far away. "You know, your grandparents bought these for him."

I imagined the soldier walking off with my horse. "*Mutter*, jacket?" I fought the urge to yank the shoes from my mother's fingers. Instead, I grabbed the pants and held out a hand. Without a word Mother passed me the shoes.

Mother tipped a finger to her lips. "Let's go to the basement."

Behind the door to our section hung an old coat Father wore when he was doing chores. "I could wash it," Mother said, inspecting the paint stain on one sleeve. "That won't come out."

"We don't have time to wash and dry," I said, fighting down my anxiety.

"At least let me darn the holes."

SIX O'CLOCK—EVENING

My stomach growled as we climbed back upstairs. I wanted to ask about dinner, about the pot on the stove. But I didn't because I knew even without opening the lid that the pot was empty—as empty as our bellies.

Mother returned to the kitchen, Siegfried and I on her heels. She hesitated, looked at us. "I suppose I better make dinner."

Right.

Siegfried rubbed his middle. "What are we having?"

Remaining silent, Mother opened the breadbox where a three-inch piece of cornbread waited. "It'll have to do."

While we took a seat at the table, Mother cut the bread into three even pieces, scraped a pea-sized amount of margarine on each and sprinkled them with sugar.

You wouldn't think you could smell a stupid piece of cornbread, but in the emptiness of that kitchen, my nose was doing overtime.

Much too fast, the bread disappeared. I downed two glasses of water and followed it up with a cup of peppermint tea Mother had warmed on the oven. She didn't say anything, but I knew she felt guilty. Once I'd overheard her talking to Father how she hated to see us hungry. She saw it as a personal failure, no matter that the madman in Berlin and the crazy Germans had caused it.

It was way too early to leave, yet my legs kept wiggling under the table. In the light of a candle stub Mother darned the jacket. The right elbow was through and there was a burn hole in the lapel. Taking a long needle and wool thread, Mother carefully covered the holes.

"Hopefully it won't show too much tonight. I'm afraid he won't be very happy with the clothes you're bringing."

I thought about the horse man who'd looked so tired and dejected. He'd not care what he wore as long as it wasn't a Wehrmacht uniform. All I needed was to have a full set he could change into and to get my hands on the horse.

The horse. What a sad-looking animal it was. It fit the man perfectly, looking just as dejected and malnourished. I thought about my birthday tomorrow, the way I'd always looked forward to celebrating. Last year, there'd been no celebration except for an extra piece of cornbread and a pair of hand-knitted gloves. By the looks of it, this year would be worse. We were even out of bread. As if to remind me, my belly rumbled.

The sugar bits were making me hungry all over again.

EIGHT O'CLOCK—EVENING

Helmut arrived looking anxious and tired. I knew his dinner had been as sparse as mine.

We set off into the dark, clothes in a tight bundle under my arm. With every step my insides got more twisted. I heard Helmut's ragged breaths next to me and knew he wasn't doing any better. I wanted nothing more than to turn around. But that would've meant admitting defeat. And my hunger didn't allow that.

After the fires had died a few weeks ago, we had no electricity, the night a shroud of black ink covering the city, while people were sitting in fear of more bomb attacks. Being outside most nights, my eyes had adjusted to pick up the slightest hint of light.

"You sure about this?" Helmut said after a while.

"Aren't you tired of being hungry?"

"Yes, but what if that officer…"

"We'll be careful."

After what seemed like an eternity, I saw something glowing: fires. Like red eyes, they showed the way, their smoke more noticeable than the light. "Not a word from now on," I whispered.

Silent as the wings of an owl, we snuck toward the barn. It was pitch black and cold as we huddled inside. I rubbed my shoulders, ordering my legs to quit trembling. It didn't work, so I slung my arms around my knees like I'd done when my brother, Hans, left for the war.

What time was it? My thoughts wandered to my brother as they did every night. And like every night, my heart grew heavy with the lack of news. Well, there was news, plenty of it, about courageous battles and fallen heroes. Since the bombing six weeks ago, the newspaper had shrunk to two pages, and without electricity the radio was no longer an option.

"What if he doesn't show?" Helmut's voice trembled.

"He'll show!" I said, struggling to sound confident. The slice of bread at dinner was a distant memory, and I was so hungry that my head felt as if it could float away in the dark. It was hard to think of anything but the ache in my gut.

"Maybe he already found clothes and is long gone," Helmut whispered, rubbing his hands together. "I'd love to have a fire. They look really nice."

I remained silent as the worry of being discovered made my throat close up. Mother was right and so was Helmut. That *Hauptmann* would shoot us on the spot. And if the SS or Gestapo found us, two civilian boys, with a military horse, we'd be dead, too. A sigh rattled the air; it was my own. I forced air into my lungs. There was still time to leave.

But I had to have the horse. I leaned against the rough-hewn wood of the barn and pulled the collar of my coat to cover my ears, the coarse wool scratching my neck. Though the dirt floor was bare, the faint smell of straw remained. Voices drifted across, too low to understand.

"You aren't sleeping?" I whispered.

How I hated the war. It had taken everything from me; at first Father, then Hans, my chance at a normal life with school and decent food—all I'd loved and known.

"No."

"What time is it?"

"No idea."

NINE O'CLOCK—EVENING

Unable to sit any longer, I jumped up and began to pace. Five steps to the wall, back the other way. "I'm going to—"

A faint noise made me freeze. Was it the soldier or was somebody else coming? Maybe a guard doing their rounds?

"You hear that?" Helmut whispered.

In that moment I heard another sound, a clunk of sorts, then another. Those had to be hooves.

Then two shadows, one large, one man-sized, appeared in the barn door.

"Boys?" Despite being whispered, the soldier's voice sounded anxious.

I jumped from my hiding place. "We brought clothes." I thrust the package at the man who consisted of shadows and seemed to have shrunken since this afternoon.

"Good." Without hesitation, the soldier undressed, the air heavy with his stench.

I listened for sounds, my insides on fire with worry. What if someone had seen the horse walk off? And why was the man taking so long? As the man fiddled with the buttons of his shirt, I tied up the uniform and handed it to him.

The soldier sighed. "You saved my life. Take care of my mare, she'll die anyway. At least you can use her." He disappeared around the corner and was gone.

I peered out after him. All was quiet. A few fires smoldered— the camp was seemingly asleep. I hoped the man would be able to flee and disappear. Everything was falling apart anyway. Deep down I wished my father and Hans would do the same. Even if it was more dangerous being a soldier, the SS never hesitated when they caught a deserter. Called 'drumhead court martials', they had the right to shoot their fellow men on the spot, even civilians, no judge or court necessary. It was happening regularly; sometimes a note would be in the paper.

Deserter caught and brought to justice.

Equally punished were people who believed in other forms of politics—like our neighbor, the communist who'd been arrested two years ago and not resurfaced since—or suggested that Germany surrendered. 'Surrender' was not in Hitler's vocabulary. He was going to take us down, no matter what.

"…ready?" Helmut's voice brought me back.

"Let's go!"

I yanked the reins. The horse didn't move. She'd witnessed battles, bleeding and dying men, walked for years without rest, slowly turning from a beautiful warhorse to skin and bones. Now she was ready to take a break.

"You pull, I'll push." I rammed my shoulder into the horse's rump. To my horror, the mare neighed. "Shh!" Through the haze of my panic, I heard voices. Somebody was coming. "Hurry."

Terror was taking my breath. I shoved harder. At last, the horse took a step… and another. We rounded the corner and stopped behind the barn when I heard movement on the other side of the barn wall.

"Nobody here." The voice was tired, kind of slow and gravelly. "I need a light."

I tiptoed to stand next to Helmut, watching the dark bulk of the horse, willing it to be quiet. My fingers shook as I stroked the horse's mane and nose. We waited. A muffled clunk reached my ear; one of the hooves had likely hit a rock. I held my breath. Though I heard nothing, I felt the presence of the men on the other side of the wall.

"Didn't Hartmann plan to put his horse into the barn?" a second voice said.

"Nothing here," the tired voice answered.

"I could've sworn he said—"

"Let's get some sleep."

As the men's steps faded away, we waited. I wanted to puke, something sour rising from my stomach. I had expected to feel triumphant, but the feeling of uneasiness remained. My throat ached with thirst. The horse next to us trembled, then rubbed her head against my shoulder.

"You think they have names?" I whispered.

"Who?"

"The warhorses."

"Doubt it," Helmut said. "They likely die too fast."

I thought about Helmut's words, those horses, animals with warm bodies and souls. Who knew, maybe they'd dreamed about spending their time on a pasture, living in a herd, rolling in the grass, maybe finding a mate. I rubbed the mare's powerful jaw.

"You had other plans, didn't you?"

"What?"

"I was talking to the horse."

Helmut scoffed. "We should go."

"Let me take a look first." Without waiting for Helmut's answer, I snuck to the corner, past the rough barn walls to the front from where I had a good view of the camp. The fires glowed; surely there were men watching. At least nobody seemed close.

"Let's go," I said as soon as I rounded the corner.

ELEVEN O'CLOCK—NIGHT

With the horse between us, we headed downhill toward our neighborhood. If anyone stopped us now, we'd be in serious trouble, accused of stealing a military horse. If the wrong person saw us, it'd mean we'd be arrested. If it were the SS or Gestapo, it'd mean execution. My coat was all of a sudden too hot and I opened the upper button.

To distract myself, I said, "You think we can go by the well? I'm burning up. The horse could probably use a drink, too."

Helmut, who was attempting to scale a pile of debris, abruptly turned around. "What's this supposed to be? The horse is going to die and you plan to water it?"

Even in my tired state, I could tell that Helmut was angry. *I don't want her to die. I want her to go onto a green meadow with lots of grass and hay and—*

"...what are we doing this for?" Helmut's voice pulled me back.

"You're right," I said. "But I need water. It's going to be a long night... and if the horse wants one last drink, she should..."

"The well it is."

I climbed next to Helmut, patted the horse's neck. "Come on, lazy, let's go."

The horse didn't feel like climbing and stood still, or maybe it sensed our raw nerves. It snorted as the heat from its breath rose between us. How did you make a horse move when it wanted to rest? But that was really a minor issue in what lay ahead. Until Helmut's words, I'd been so focused on getting the horse and safely

36

taking it home that I'd not thought of what would follow. I'd been running on empty all day and felt drained, my legs like jelly and my mind fuzzy. No wonder the horse refused to continue. It had to be exhausted and probably missed its owner.

In this moment I understood what we would have to do. I'd told Mother I could take care of the slaughter and that I'd bring home food. There was no backing out.

"We have to find another path." Helmut sounded tired and frustrated.

"What?"

"Are you listening?"

I heaved a sigh. "*Ja, Mann*. Let's go past the hedges."

As we pulled on the reins, the horse whinnied again. I listened in fright, feeling powerless. If we gave up, we'd lose the horse, our chance for real food. We had to trust that nobody was up at this hour.

I patted the horse's neck again. "Come on, you can do it. Let's get some water."

Rocks clinked below as the old mare began to move.

I breathed a sigh of relief when we reached the well. It was always a bit spooky here, the little pointed well house like a silent soldier guarding the water. From its side wall spewed a steady stream of icy water into a stone trough that emptied into a pond. As I drank and cooled my burning forehead, the horse slurped in noisy gulps. Had I just been here this morning? It seemed like a lifetime had passed.

The water spread frosty fingers through my middle. My mind was playing tricks now, the edges of my vision like a black frame closing in. I knew it was my stomach demanding to be filled. All that running around was taking its toll.

TWELVE O'CLOCK—MIDNIGHT

We agreed to try the old community kitchen near my apartment house and headed off again. My ears were on high alert, but all I noticed were our breaths and the clunk of hooves.

The one-story building that housed the community washhouse was used by everyone in the neighborhood. I knew it would be deserted. Since the bombing there was no water, and people washed only what was absolutely necessary—underwear and socks—because they had to carry every drop of water nearly a kilometer.

Shoving and pushing, we dragged the horse inside. Despite it being pitch black, I knew the room was filthy, but it had tile walls and a drain in the floor. I lit the small candle I carried for emergencies, its shine barely reaching five feet across. I could make out the horse's front feet, the walls beyond hidden in shadow.

"Maybe we should wait till morning." Helmut sagged on a turned-over zinc tub. "I'm bushed."

I wanted to slump next to him, find a way to delay the inevitable. "And do what?" It came out like a nasty accusation.

"Sleep here and watch the horse." Helmut obviously ignored my aggressive tone.

"Someone will see us." I rubbed my arms and legs to fend off the creeping cold that had followed us inside. The horse snorted and watched as if to remind me that I wanted nothing more than to run and forget about the whole thing. But waiting was not going to do anything except make the task harder. The longer we stayed here, the closer I'd grow to the old mare.

This was going to be a horrific job. It wasn't just that I was bone tired—the idea of killing an animal, not to mention a huge beast, made me faint with worry.

As long I could remember I'd enjoyed nature, accompanying my father into the woods, watching squirrels and birds, hiking cross-country, enjoying the spicy fall air, saving earthworms from drowning by moving them into the dirt. Every creature had a right to be here, to share this earth with us. But the rules had changed. Everything about my life was different thanks to Hitler who'd put us into this mess and forced us to do unmentionable things just to stay alive. Despite the cold, I felt hot with hatred for this little man lying to us and the fact that I felt utterly helpless to do anything about it.

We needed food, period, or we'd lie down and starve to death like some of our elderly neighbors. Why couldn't my father be here to help? Or Hans? I shook off the image of them lying in some ditch, forgotten and covered with weeds.

When I rubbed the mare's long and coarse mane, the soft skin beneath her ears, she snorted and moved her head up and down as if she were talking to me. What had we gotten ourselves into? Mother was right, of course. This was no chicken or rabbit, not even a pig. This animal was huge and even in its current run-down state would require a lot of force to kill.

"I'm sure you are just as hungry as we are," I mumbled. Massaging my stiff neck, I nodded toward Helmut. "We need a hammer."

"What for?"

"The horse, you idiot. Unless you've got a gun in your pocket."

"No need to get mad. We have a hammer in the basement." Helmut stretched his long arms and stood up.

"A big one," I called after him. "And more light."

TWELVE-THIRTY—EARLY MORNING

I leaned my face against the mare's neck. She smelled of horse, kind of warm and comfortable, and when she began to nibble on the sleeve of my jacket, I realized how peaceful she made me feel. How was that even possible?

I rubbed her chest, a mottled brownish red, caked with mud. "How dirty you are." The horse snorted. I wondered what she understood. My fingers found a patch of bare skin, an old wound, still pink and shiny. "Looks like you are a veteran, too."

For a brief moment, I wondered if Helmut would chicken out and not return. What nonsense! He was always by my side and no matter how hard things got, he was my friend. I trusted him, even if he sometimes made me mad. Not because he was wrong or said things I disagreed with. Just the opposite. He voiced his concerns openly, the same ones I had and kept to myself. I realized that Helmut was a lot braver than I, because he was not afraid to say things out loud, while I tended to bury my feelings.

The horse neighed, and its hooves clunked softly on the concrete floor. To distract myself, I kept rubbing the coarse fur, running my fingers along the neck to its withers. The skin was broken in places where the saddle had been. Surely it felt pain from its wounds. By the state of her protruding ribs and hip bones, she'd been hungry for months.

"What have you seen and done?" I asked.

Of course, there was no answer. I had no idea what breed she was, her age, or where she had lived before the war. The Wehrmacht used lots of horses, some to ride, some to pull carts and artillery. Only one thing was clear: this animal had seen a lot—too much. It was malnourished and downtrodden, but worse was that it had no spirit left. Hitler had taken that too. The horse was like us: worn thin and disheartened—waiting for the end.

And *I* was one of the *lucky* ones. Though they'd mustered us a few months ago, I'd not been drafted yet. I was sleeping in my own bed, unlike my brother, Hans, and Father, who likely sat in some ditch, waiting to be shot down.

A sigh escaped me. It had to be late... after midnight. Today was my sixteenth birthday. I may not be an adult, but even I knew that this war was going nowhere. We were defeated, the country bled out. Father had told us in whispered tones about the state of their unit, that they had hardly any ammunition, and neither uniforms nor what they wore underneath was being replaced. I'd seen the same look in the men who'd walked uphill earlier today, their defeat and exhaustion. How much longer was Hitler going to keep this up? To what end?

How many more had to die—at the front or in prison camps, in their beds during a bomb raid, or because they'd lost the will to live?

With my forehead leaning against the mare's neck, I closed my eyes and dozed, wishing for this impossible night to be over.

TWO O'CLOCK—EARLY MORNING

A noise roused me and it took me a moment to figure out where I was. The horse neighed softly as Helmut appeared in the shine of the candle, dragging a sledgehammer behind him along with a hand-wagon, a wood contraption with squeaky iron wheels.

"Sorry, it took a while. I had to be quiet. But I got knives, too." He panted as if we'd just stopped talking a minute ago.

I unfolded a stack of precious newspaper and within lay three large and two paring knives next to an enamel bowl, wrapped in a towel.

The moment of truth had arrived. I could no longer pretend that I was rescuing a horse; just the opposite.

"Who is going to do it?" Helmut asked. The skin on his forehead shimmered damp despite the frigid air.

"I don't know." My resolve had evaporated. Despite her sad state, the mare was huge. Again, she neighed softly as if she wanted to ask us what we were thinking.

Helmut's eyes looked huge in his pale face. "Maybe we should draw straws? The shorter stick loses."

"Fine."

"Fine."

Helmut returned with a grass blade and tore it into two sections. "You first."

I swallowed hard as I grabbed a piece from his hand. Helmut's arm shook as he slowly opened his fist. I sighed—on my palm rested the shorter piece.

I gingerly lifted the hammer and let it sink to the floor. With a three-foot handle, it felt heavy as a boulder.

"Did you see her scars?" I said. "Look at this." A second scar, long and covered with coarse scab, stretched along the horse's hind leg. "I wonder what happened." I traced a finger across her flank.

"Are we going to do this or not?"

"I'm getting to it," I hissed, my voice foreign and tinny like speaking into a barrel. I tried to look away, away from the gentle brown eyes and away from the soft nose. I had to do this now. Before I went crazy or ran off. Mother and Siegfried needed to eat. We all needed to eat. "I'll climb on the counter. Bring her over."

"Wait!" Helmut shouted. "Cover her eyes."

"Good idea. Hand me that rag you brought." Anything to avoid standing here thinking about what I was about to do. Climbing on a broken piece of countertop at the back of the room, I bound the towel around the horse's head. "Now the hammer."

Helmut handed it over. He'd lit another candle stub so we'd be able to see what we were doing. Except I didn't want to look nor think about this horror of a task. The sledgehammer had a mind of its own as I swung it back and forth. It felt impossible to maneuver; my arms were drained. *Do it*, my mind urged. *Now.*

I gripped the hammer tighter and swallowed, my mouth dry as the desert. My stomach was making weird noises. Was I hungry or about to throw up?

"One, two and three." I closed my eyes.

The horse stood quietly as the hammer hit her forehead with a sickening thud. Something cracked deep inside. A muffled sound crept from the horse's throat; not a whinny or a snort, more like a gurgle. Hooves scraped concrete as her bowels gave and the room filled with the stink of fresh manure.

Helmut's voice drifted into my fogged brain, but I couldn't make out what he was saying. *Quickly,* my mind urged.

I swung with all I'd left. The hammer missed the forehead and slammed into its brow. Blood spurted, skin tore, splattering Helmut's face. Whitish bone fragments appeared in the red mass above the eye. The hammer crashed between the mare's ears.

The mare trembled, ripples traveling through her body. Then, in slow motion, her feet gave, her front knees buckled, then her hind legs. She tilted sideways and fell, her bulk filling the room, her head hitting the tile. She lay still, but I heard her labored breathing as loud as that Wehrmacht truck with the fanatic officer. Blood oozed from her nose. I jumped down and grabbed one of the knives.

"Get the bowl. She must die quickly." I cut the horse's neck as Helmut shoved the bowl below. Blood spewed, covering us in a slimy spray of red. A puddle grew on the cement. Crimson rivulets snaked toward the drain in the middle of the floor.

"Man, that stinks." Helmut held his nose, leaving a bloody print on his face.

"The bowl, hold it close," I shouted. I was no longer myself, just some strange being, existing in an undefinable space, my mind filled with darkness, a black hole of despair. Bile filled my throat. Helmut tried to keep the bowl steady, but the blood poured fast and hard, drenched our skin, clothes and shoes. The bowl filled and spilled over. The horse seemed to have buckets.

I wanted to make sure she was really dead and crawled on top of her neck which felt warm and still soft. *Don't lose it now.*

There was no pulse.

THREE O'CLOCK—EARLY MORNING

"She's gone," I whispered. Was that really my voice? I took a deep breath, regretted it immediately because the mix of blood and manure made me gag. It was as if death was choking me, reminding me of what I'd done. *Think of Mother and Siegfried; think how happy they'll be. Father would also be proud. He'd do it too if it meant survival.*

When I finally rose, Helmut thrust the largest knife at me. It was slightly rusty but very sharp with a curved blade and a pointed tip. "Let's pull her guts out first." The way he said it, his voice all pinched and hoarse, I knew he was just as disgusted and anxious as I was.

Why me? I wanted to say. *Why don't you continue and leave me alone?* Too tired to argue, I made the first cut along the stomach, then another. Bile shot up my throat. I gagged as the knife dug deep and separated the layers of skin, exposing grayish intestines.

I took hold of the hide, attempting to pull it apart. Instead, my fingers slipped on the gunky mess. I wiped my fingers on my pants and croaked, "Help me!"

Together we tucked and pulled, arms deep inside the steaming belly, guts spilling onto concrete. I heard Helmut's gurgled swallows, my own stomach threatening to turn. I had to numb my senses; not think, not now.

I kept pulling, wishing to lose my sense of smell. It was no good. The stench infiltrated my brain, making every breath a chore. Intestines slithered across the floor, seemingly endless whitish strings of entrails transforming the air into a thick, steamy mass. The formerly white walls were splattered red, the floor unrecognizable.

We shoved everything to the side so we could work and get to the meat.

"I'll start with the backside." I pushed the knife against the skin along the croup and cut along the spine, my breath ragged. More blood oozed from the cut. "Get the paper ready."

"I'm right here," Helmut said, unfolding a large sheet of newspaper. "Don't you have to remove the skin first? I used to help my father with the rabbits and we always skinned them first."

"Right. Hand me that shorter knife." I sliced across the back, starting at the neck, along the spine all the way to the dock where the tail started, telling myself that it was just a piece of meat like the butcher had sold us a thousand times—before the war, before all this madness. "Here, grab hold of this." The skin resisted, slipped beneath my fingers. Everything was slimy and smelled. "You pull while I cut."

Slowly, we worked our way along the back, down one side until the mare's flank was exposed, its meat the brownish red of old wine. I wiped my fingers once more, regripped the knife and began to cut.

"Take this." Holding up a first chunk, I felt half triumphant. This was lifesaving food, I told myself, avoiding looking to my left, where the mare's head lay still. I'd left the rag on her eyes as if she could watch what I was doing.

Helmut gingerly touched the meat, still warm and seemingly alive. "It's slippery."

I ignored him and cut another piece. "What are you waiting for? Here's another."

"I'm getting it." Helmut grabbed the piece more firmly and wrapped newspaper around it. "I hate this smell."

We kept going in silence, me cutting and Helmut wrapping and storing on the cart.

"I don't think the wagon can hold any more," he said after a while.

I wiped my sweaty face. "We better take a break so we can take this home. You go first."

We'd agreed to take turns delivering the meat to our mothers. With that much food, we'd have to make several runs.

My right wrist ached and my fingers cramped, so I rose from the backbreaking work and took a deep breath. The entire room seemed to glow crimson, the tile floor covered under entrails, bits of meat, hide and blood, lots of blood.

My arms were covered in it, the sleeves of my sweater soaked. Luckily, I'd taken off my coat, though now I felt the cold creep in once more. All I wanted was to finish and go home, bury my head beneath my comforter and sleep for two days.

For a moment I considered asking Mother to help, but that was out of the question. She was a small woman, and I would spare her seeing and smelling this bloodbath.

With a sigh I returned to the horse's rump. I was carving up a portion of the back and hind leg when the door opened and Helmut reappeared with the wagon. Though I'd expected him, my breath caught in fright.

THREE-THIRTY—EARLY MORNING

Catching myself, I said, "You want to take over for a while." It wasn't meant as a question. I needed air.

Not waiting for an answer, I marched outside, breathing deeply, the stickiness on my skin turning to instant frost. The sky was clear now and sparkled with stars, hard lights like crystals; a thin moon added soft light. It had to be several degrees below freezing and ordinarily I would've enjoyed the view. Now all I wanted was for this night to be over. With a shudder I forced myself to turn back.

Helmut was bent over the horse's back, packing the second load. "This one is ready. We've got at least four more runs. You're next—"

"What are you boys up to?" A man hovered in the shadows of the entrance. I'd seen him before, somewhere in the neighborhood, but didn't know his name. Inches shorter than us, he stared from watery eyes whose color was hard to guess. He was older than Father, his face puffy and soft, shining pale like kneaded dough.

In my gut, warning bells began to ring. Why wasn't the man in the war? He didn't seem to have any obvious injuries. But then I knew there were always some who managed to escape the draft or weaseled away from the front. Most of the time, these men had connections to the SS or Gestapo. They were cheap spies who turned in their neighbors for an extra ration.

Until a few years ago, we'd had a neighbor who'd been a communist. Father said somebody had turned him in and one day, a black car stopped on the street to arrest him. Nobody had seen him since.

"We butchered a horse," Helmut said, pulling me back to the present.

"A horse, eh." The man glanced at the carcass on the floor. "Did you steal it?" He licked his lips like a hungry animal. They were dark with flakes of skin in the corners as if he'd chewed his mouth. His chest and shoulders appeared bowed, making him appear hunched underneath the oversized coat.

"We traded it fairly." Helmut placed himself between the horse and the door—knife, dripping with blood, firmly in his hand.

"Not likely—two boys getting a horse like this." The man's eyes spoke of greed as he glanced at the meat on the wagon, the uncarved front and shoulder. "Maybe I should call the authorities." He tried straightening and bounced on his heels to look important.

I sighed, stepping next to my friend. "Look, *Herr*... We traded the horse as we told you. You know us, we live down the street."

"Nobody gives a couple of boys a horse. I think you stole that horse from our military, a serious offense."

Who are you to question us, I wanted to scream. Aloud I said, "We didn't." My voice shook, but I grabbed the other knife. Cold anger spread as I watched the small man eyeing *our* meat. Even at my age, I'd seen his kind before—opportunists who stole from their own mothers to get ahead.

"You know my father, Artur Schmidt?" I said, wishing I were strong and tall. "And my grandfather, Egon—he owned the scissor factory."

"So what?" the man said. We were silent for a moment, looking at each other. "Give me some pieces or I'll report you."

Helmut looked at me and we nodded to each other.

"Sure." I straightened my shoulders, looking at my bloodstained hands. "We'll give you the bones."

"Bones? Give me meat or I'll go to the SS right now." The man smiled for the first time. "You're lucky I didn't get here earlier. I'll be back in a few and you better be gone by then." Without waiting for a reply, he disappeared.

"*Scheisse*," I said. "I wish we could carry her off."

"You think he'll report us?"

"Doubt it. He wants the meat. *Our* meat," I growled.

"Let's hurry then," Helmut said, returning to the carcass. I joined him and wordlessly we continued cutting. Only now it was a race against an enemy who was lurking on our own street, a German who was going to steal from a couple of boys.

"We need another cart, this one is already overloaded."

"I don't want to leave you," I said, having visions of Helmut being attacked by the small man. Who knew, maybe he was getting his friends right this minute to overwhelm us.

"How about we hide some of it outside?" Helmut rubbed his lower back. "We can get it later."

"Good idea."

FOUR O'CLOCK—EARLY MORNING

We rushed outside to look for a suitable hiding place. The world seemed to consist of shadows and black voids, ready to swallow us, the thin moon low now, the air enveloping us with icy arms. I spotted the opening of a coal cellar, a square hole next to a house. Its wooden top was missing, likely stolen to use as firewood. I scanned the shadows. Was anyone out there? Did the little man watch us from some window? More likely he was getting his knives and cart ready to steal our food. Quickly, we stashed the meat and returned. One of the candles had burned out, so the light was even dimmer now.

Silently, we returned to carving and wrapping as quickly as we could. Just minutes ago, I'd wished myself home into my bed, but now I was ready to fight for my rights. This mare had died for us. I'd looked into her eyes, had spoken to her, tried to tell her how sorry I was. Now some thief was threatening us.

I doubted he'd call the SS to investigate, but one could never be sure; nothing was a given these days. Normal laws didn't apply. People did what they deemed necessary to survive. Others took Hitler's world order to enrich and empower themselves, often at the cost of the small people—us.

My ears were on high alert as we filled another wagon. The back rump had been cut away and we needed to turn the carcass on its other side. The animal was still huge and filled out most of the space.

"Let's try to turn her," I said, wiping my damp brow. By now we had to look like we'd been in a massacre, but there was no time to clean up.

"I'll stash the meat first," Helmut said. "That man will be back, I'm sure of it."

Back inside, Helmut grabbed the stiffened hindlegs while I picked up the front ones. I was so exhausted now, I could hardly feel my arms, and the ache in my back and shoulders had increased to a dull throb. *Not much longer*, I told myself.

Inch by inch we rocked the horse to the other side, where Helmut immediately began to cut away the hide.

"You're still here." His voice was quiet now, but full of menace.

"We'll take what is ours." I looked up from the carcass, the knife heavy in my hand. "We'll finish this piece and fill the wagon. Then we'll go."

The man squinted, something wild in his eyes. He opened his coat to reveal an axe and a large knife, and he lit a couple of candle stubs. "Get out of here, before I miss." He swung the axe in a wide arch, forcing me to jump back.

Helmut cowered behind the rump, eyeing the blade as it sank deep into the horse's shoulder. On the second try the axe hit concrete. Sparks pierced the gloom. The man began to move quickly, sending chunks of bone and meat flying.

I flinched. "Hurry," I whispered, keeping my gaze on the swinging axe. We cut along the back end as the axe moved closer. We had nowhere to go.

"We are leaving," I hissed, piling the last chunks of meat on the wagon.

The man didn't look up. He was severing the front leg. "Good, and don't come back."

We pulled out quickly and as I gripped my knife, fresh heat bubbled up in my veins. Never before had I wished to be grown as much as tonight. Never before had I wished so much to have my father home. In a last move, I blew out my candle and held it to let it harden. I waited a moment until Helmut went outside, then I quickly blew out the nasty man's candles and slipped through the door.

Cursing erupted behind me, but I only smiled grimly as I helped Helmut pull away the cart.

FIVE-THIRTY—MORNING

"He's stealing our food," I huffed as we dragged the cart down the street.

"I wish my father were here," Helmut said. "Both our fathers. They'd beat him up."

I imagined Father marching down to the kitchen and grabbing the little man by his neck. He'd shake him a bit before giving him a swift kick out the door. "I'll remember him. When all this is over, I'll remember him."

"If it ever *is* over."

"It has to. How much longer can we keep up when our own men have nothing to fight with?"

Helmut didn't answer, but I knew he was thinking about his own father.

The chunks of meat wrapped in newspaper still quivered as we turned into my street. Nothing moved yet, our neighbors no doubt dreading another day, to rise having little to eat and even less to heat with. And to think that Christmas was only four days away.

We stopped in front of our house where Helmut waited while I loaded my arms with meat and climbed to the second floor.

"I've got more downstairs," I announced when the door opened.

Mother's eyes grew large as she clapped a hand over her mouth. "Oh no, what happened? Where are you hurt? I was so worried."

I grimaced. "It's horse blood. Today we'll eat well."

Mother's face lit up as she exclaimed, "Thank goodness, look at

53

all this food."

"We would've had a lot more. A man stole it all. I wish *Vater* were here." To my embarrassment, my throat tightened. I angrily wiped my eyes with a blood-soaked sleeve. "I better go and get the rest. Helmut is waiting downstairs."

SIX O'CLOCK—MORNING

Under the cover of darkness, we hurried back and forth until we had retrieved the remainder of the meat. Helmut disappeared with a wagon load full, his face pale and drawn. All we did was nod to each other... for a job well done, for helping each other, for being friends and dealing with an unspeakable task. Without Helmut I couldn't have done it.

Upstairs Mother put an arm around my shoulder as she glanced around the kitchen where the table, counters and bench held packages of horse meat. "You did it, Günter, you really did it." She shook her head and embraced my face with her hands. "I'm proud of you. I didn't think it was possible."

I just smiled at her, wanted to tell her about the nasty man, but I had no energy.

"I'll set up the grinder. You better fetch my largest pot." Mother threw me another glance. "On second thought, why don't you wash? We still have clean water in the bucket." She looked at my shoes that looked like I'd been in a battle. "I'll worry about those later."

Most of the blood had dried on my skin, so I pulled off my shirt and pants to soak in the remaining water and began to scrub until it hurt. In a way the pain felt good... No, it felt right—I deserved it.

I took out my good set kept for Sundays as the smell of frying meat reached my nostrils. It was a smell I hardly remembered, rich and flavorful. Saliva formed in my mouth, forced me to swallow. I could finally eat. Somehow, I'd expected to feel elated, but all I felt was exhaustion that went bone deep... and sadness.

"Here," Mother said as soon as I entered the kitchen and placed a plate of raw ground meat in front of me. "Just promise me to eat slowly or you'll get sick. When you're done, I'll need help cutting wood for the stove. We'll fry these patties and can the rest."

As I slowly chewed, Siegfried came running into the kitchen. "What is that?"

"Horse meat," I said quietly.

Still in his pajamas, he slid next to me and picked a piece from my plate. "Hmm, that's tasty."

"You get your own, Siegfried." Mother placed a plate with a second portion in front of him. "Just chew it well." As she turned toward me, she suddenly cried out, "Oh, my goodness." In a swift move, she embraced me from behind, saying, "Happy birthday. With all this excitement, I'd forgotten."

I smiled at my mother and patted her arm. "It's all right. At least we've got enough food for a while."

"I don't have much to give you." Mother straightened and handed me a pair of wool socks, undoubtedly knitted with wool from old sweaters.

"Thank you. I don't need much." It was true, I didn't. The mare had sacrificed herself; she was my gift, a gift I could share with my family, the only important thing in my life.

SEVEN-THIRTY—MORNING

We covered the front door with blankets to avoid alerting any neighbors who would be attracted to the smell like bees to nectar. It didn't matter that we didn't have any oil or butter, eggs or spices. Burger patties piled a foot high on plates and canning jars lined the table.

By the time I went to bed, I was utterly drained, my legs and arms like mush, my back and shoulders tight knots. My stomach was full for once, but I couldn't enjoy it. Had it only been twenty-four hours since I'd gotten up to begin a desperate search for food? The entire day and night knitted together in a thick unruly glob like wool boiled in water. I'd turned a year older, but nothing made sense anymore: not our lives in this downtrodden, ruined city, and not where the country was heading, sending my father and brother to their deaths.

I'd killed an innocent horse who'd served a soldier for years; had enabled his escape. I loved animals, but instead of honoring her, I'd cut her to shreds and given her up to some low-life thug. The war was turning us all into animals: Hitler, the SS and Gestapo, the men at the front, the bombers, spying neighbors and now me—a murderer of horses. I turned on my side, bitter tears in my throat.

The last thing I saw was a pair of brown eyes with long lashes.

EPILOGUE

JUNE 15, 2021

I often think back to that day in 1944 when I did something I'd never thought possible. It is strange how these memories are so real now, more real than this present life of mine at the age of ninety-two. I'm old, my body weak and shrunken. I'm sitting on my swing in the garden, listening to the birds and watching the goldfish in the pond I dug forty years ago. It is pretty much all I can do these days, sit and think… Reminisce about a time long gone. It's the prerogative of old age to do nothing productive and not feel the slightest bit guilty about it.

I'm old, but in my memories everything is as clear and fresh as the day it happened. When I tell people about this time, they look at me in disbelief. They cannot comprehend what it was like to have nothing to eat. Nothing. To feel hungry to a point where the mind played tricks, turned everyday tasks like chopping wood into seemingly insurmountable chores.

How could they? We have grocery stores at every corner and most people in our Western societies can choose between fifteen types of pasta, select from dozens of cheeses and meats, not to mention the insane variety of breads. Salt and sugar are cheap staples, and we throw away what appears to be the slightest bit stale or out of date.

I on the other hand cannot bring myself to throw away food. Not even moldy bread. I cut the bad parts away and chew the hard edges, even if my teeth can hardly keep up. My daughters scold me, tell me it is unhealthy. Too bad! I'm ninety-two years old. I survived the war as a child and youth, survived my beloved wife, Helga, by seventeen years. A little mold doesn't scare me.

What I do want people to understand, even my children, is that nobody can truly comprehend the horror of the last months of the war. Maybe it wasn't so bad for the big men on top—though I doubt that today—but we kids and remaining families were pushed to the edge of sanity.

Rightly so, many of you will say. Didn't Hitler kill six million Jews, snuff out minorities and bomb many countries, killing innocent civilians? He did and I'm ashamed for my country, ashamed of the many men and women who supported him.

In the end, he and his cronies killed not only those mentioned, but millions of their own countrymen and even children because they couldn't stand the idea of losing. They rather planned to destroy what was left of Germany before they gave in.

No matter, the war has been over for more than seventy-five years. And I think we *can* agree that war is never the answer. Never!

So, I ask you what you would've done, had you been in my shoes. Would you have continued starving or would you have killed that soldier's horse?

And to answer your other question, yes, my father and Hans, my brother, returned home in the summer of 1945: my father on foot from the Balkans, strong and seemingly unharmed, Hans emaciated as a skeleton with loose teeth and skin so black it took weeks to scrub him clean. We were one of the lucky ones, an intact family again, though the trauma of the war remained with us for a lifetime.

Günter 2021

Günter, ca. 1947

AUTHOR NOTE

Hunger

Hunger is a primary human instinct, designed to keep us alive. Hunger causes stomach growling and pain, low energy, shakiness, headaches and problems focusing. Prolonged hunger also leads to irritation and depression, hypertension and anemia. Hunger alters perception and may lead the affected to take greater risks.

We all have seen reports of survivors who, stranded in some unknown or hostile territory, did incredible things to stay alive. They collected bugs and worms, ate whatever animals they could catch, and in some instances, resorted to cannibalism.

People who have always enjoyed full refrigerators and cupboards do not know what hunger is or what it does to the body and mind—this author included. In the industrialized Western world, hunger is also present, but mostly remains hidden in shame.

My father had met hunger not just once. Hunger had been his companion for years, crept up on him in 1943 und remained by his side until June 20, 1948, the day the Deutsch Mark was introduced and ended black markets and food shortages.

Horses in the Military

Horses have been used in warfare for thousands of years. They were responsible for carrying riders to patrol, fight or scout, and pulling supply carts and artillery. In the American Civil War, they played a huge role, and even during the invasion into Afghanistan in 2001, the US military used horses in battle.

In World War II, the German Wehrmacht utilized 2.8 million horses, of which more than sixty percent were killed or died of disease or malnutrition.

Horses as Food

In the US the slaughter of horses was banned in 2007 and consumption of horse meat is prohibited, though several states, such as Texas, breed horses for export to be slaughtered in Canada and Mexico. In Europe and Asia, horses are butchered for meat to this day.

The author is vegetarian and wishes that all human consumption of animal products would stop or at least be significantly reduced. Cattle, sheep, and fowl are often raised under terrible conditions in order to feed us or other animals.

TIMELINE

September 25, 1944
Hitler orders the creation of the Volkssturm, the people's storm, consisting of all able-bodied men between sixteen and sixty years of age.
October 18, 1944
Official announcement of the Volkssturm. The first participants are organized and used for propaganda purposes.
March 5, 1945
In the desperate last wave of the Volkssturm, Wilhelm Keitel, general and head of the German Wehrmacht, adds all boys born in 1929 to join the Volkssturm.
April 16/17, 1945
American troops arrive in Solingen. Its citizens surrender without a fight.
April 21, 1945
Battle of Berlin; 2.5 million Red Army soldiers surround the city, fighting one million German soldiers. The last fanatics, SS Hitler Youth, create stand-up desertion tribunals, shooting surrendering German citizens on the spot.
April 30, 1945
Hitler commits suicide.
May 2-8, 1945
The German government surrenders, and World War II in Europe ends.

MAIN CHARACTERS

Günter 1928–2021

Günter became a master dye maker and ran his own company for seven years. In 1970, he joined Hugo Pott, a world-renowned silverware company, and became a lead designer. His unique expertise, a combination of artistry and technical knowledge, made him a sought-after craftsman all his life. In his free time, he created metal and wood sculptures of animals and human forms. He had two children with his wife, Helga, the author and a second girl, and retired at age seventy. Always figuring he'd be the first to die, he was devastated when Helga fell ill. After her death, he struggled to find meaning in his life, but the grit that accompanied him all his life saved him. He remained independent and lived in the same house until three days before his death.

Helmut 1928–1992
Helmut became a typesetter and had two children with his wife, also called Helga. A heavy smoker all his life, he contracted lung cancer and passed away in 1992. Günter and Helmut remained casual friends all their lives.

ABOUT THE AUTHOR

Perhaps Annette Oppenlander became a writer of historical novels because she likes to dig in the past. It all started when she asked her parents about their experiences as war children. Over many years, these emotional memories developed into the biographical novel "Surviving the Fatherland." Not only did this story win many awards, it also served as the springboard to a successful writing career.

Ms. Oppenlander likes to shed light on difficult subjects such as World War II from the perspective of civilian Germany, walks alongside ordinary people in the American Civil War or the Middle Ages. To create an authentic historical world, she often uses biographical information, interviews contemporary witnesses and unearths little known facts in the archives.

After studying business administration at the University of Cologne, Germany, Ms. Oppenlander spent 30 years in various parts of the United States. She writes her novels in German and English, and also shares her knowledge – writing workshops, entertaining presentations and author visits to universities and schools, libraries, retirement homes and organizations dedicated to literature – in

German and English. She now lives with her American husband and dog Zelda in the beautiful Münsterland in Germany.

"Nearly every place holds some kind of secret, something that makes history come alive. When we scrutinize people and places closely, history is no longer a date or number, it turns into a story."

From the Author

Thank you for reading '24 Hours: The Trade.' My sincere hope is that you derived as much entertainment from reading this story as I enjoyed in researching and creating it. If you have a few moments, please feel free to add your review of the book at your favorite online site for feedback (Amazon, Apple iTunes Store, Goodreads, etc.). Also, if you would like to connect with previous or upcoming books, please visit my website for information and to sign up for e-news: http://www.annetteoppenlander.com.

Sincerely, Annette

Contact Me

Website: annetteoppenlander.com
Facebook: www.facebook.com/annetteoppenlanderauthor
Email: hello@annetteoppenlander.com
Instagram: @annette.oppenlander
Twitter: @aoppenlander
Pinterest: @annoppenlander

READING SAMPLE

High on the mountain on the border between Germany's states of Thuringia and Hessia perch the ruins of Castle (Burg) Hanstein, I visited in 2012. Immediately inspired by its medieval charm, I decided to write a time-travel adventure about a young gamer—Max.

"...will grip the reader's total attention from beginning to end. Very highly recommended for school and community library..." - **Midwest Book Review**

"...an entertaining and fast-paced read that guarantees to thrill any young reader's/gamer's wish to be a hero in a faraway time." -**Historical Novel Society**

When nerd and gamer, Max Anderson, is lured into trying an experimental computer game, he doesn't realize he's playing the ultimate history game, time-traveling into the past...anywhere...anytime. Survival is optional. To return home he must decipher the game's rules and complete its missions—if he lives long enough—to fail means staying in the past-forever.

Now he's trapped in medieval Germany, unprepared and clueless. It is the year 1471 and he quickly learns that being an outcast may cost him his head. Especially after rescuing a beautiful peasant girl from a deadly infection and thus provoking sinister wannabe Duke Ott. Overnight he is dragged into a hornets' nest of feuding lords who will stop at nothing to bring down the conjuring stranger in their midst.

Escape from the Past
The Duke's Wrath

CHAPTER ONE

It was exactly 9:32 pm when I settled into my favorite chair, the one with the ripped Mexican blanket that serves as a cushion. Little did I know I'd be gone within the hour. I mean gone as in disappeared.

Powering up my high-speed Cyber Xtreme and 32-inch monitor, a guilt gift from my dad and the only valuable thing I own, I stared at the blank disc in my hand. According to my friend, Jimmy, it contained some secret new game his father had invented. Jimmy said his dad thought the game had a glitch and I wondered why his dad would have given it to him.

Most people consider Jimmy the lucky one. He lives in a mansion because his father runs some ginormous tech company. My mom and me share space with a thousand spiders in a two-bedroom cottage with a thatched roof. Who in the twenty-first century lives in a house covered with a bunch of straw?

Anyway, I digress. The tower purred as it swallowed the disc, the best sound in the world. It took a long time to boot which should've given me the first clue something was wrong. If there's one thing that drives me crazy it's slow processors and I knew it wasn't my equipment. I've been gaming since I was six and consider myself pretty good. Especially when it comes to debugging stuff. I was stoked to figure it out, maybe make a few bucks in the process. I'm still American enough to think of dollars instead of Euros because we've only been living in Germany for two years.

I was scrounging for a candy bar in my desk when a flame shot across the screen, burning yellow, red and blue. Not that I smoke, but it looked real enough to light a cigarette. In slow motion the fire edged letters into the screen. *EarthRider.* Cool name. Of course, I didn't get it then. Stupid me.

Below the fire appeared a globe, the kind librarians have on their desks. The thing rotated slowly, zooming closer and closer like *Google Earth*. Jimmy was right. This was the coolest thing I'd ever seen, the graphics as realistic as if I'd been standing there. *Bornhagen*, the village we live in, was marked with a front door. *Enter here* flashed below.

I was pretty fed up waiting, my fingers twitching to hit the keys. First it took ages to load, then it showed a map? But I didn't have much else to do except review a few algebra problems—unlike Jimmy I've got no trouble with math—so I clicked.

On the screen, giant boulders shaped themselves into a gate, opening onto a bunch of hills and a shadowy forest. In the distance, high on the mountain, I saw a castle with two towers, a pale banner fluttering limply on top. It looked vaguely familiar, but at the time I didn't really think much about it. An ox cart moved slowly across a country road toward the castle.

I sniffed. Something reeked like boiled manure. I looked around to find the source when I noticed a man on the screen scurrying along a bumpy trail. He wheezed, dragging his bare feet. He was obviously injured, the filthy rags on his right shoulder dark with blood. The screen zoomed to follow as the man darted into the woods. Giant oaks swallowed the sun, a patchwork of shadows and light in the undergrowth. At the time I remember thinking how lame this game was despite the graphics—no dragons, no monsters, nothing exciting whatsoever.

Besides, I was slightly worried my mom would come in. The whiskey she likes usually puts her to sleep on the couch, but you never know. Luckily, most of the time, she doesn't realize when I pull an all-nighter.

Horse gallop thudded out of nowhere. Visibly trembling, the grimy-looking man hesitated for a moment before thrashing his way through bushes and undergrowth. At the edge of the forest three riders in chainmail and helmets came into view, their chestnut horses covered in sweat and whinnying. The clang of metal sliced the air as the men drew swords.

At that moment my cell rang. I remember hesitating because I thought maybe Jimmy's dad had found out about me borrowing the game. I'd sort of pushed for it. I should've stopped what I was doing right then, but I was still curious and decided to ignore the phone. On the screen a yellowed scroll, its edges burned and crumbling, unfolded into a menu.

Continue Level One

Expert

Pause

Exit

Upgrade to Expert now? flashed below. Cool. There was an advanced version. I moved the mouse and clicked. Instantly the screen began to pulse and recede. Like looking into a fish tank, the tree trunks, oak leaves and bushes grew larger and three-dimensional, sharper and closer. I heard birds chirping and rustling in the undergrowth. And the foul smell was back.

I leaned forward because all of a sudden my chest was killing me. I was stuck in a truck-sized vise, my ribs squeezing together, body compressing. My lungs throbbed and I couldn't breathe, not even a little. My arms and legs felt numb. *Do something*, I thought. I pushed myself to stand. *Something is wrong with the game, stop the game,* my mind urged. But I couldn't. Lights exploded behind my eyelids and I had to pay every shred of attention to the task of breathing.

It occurred to me that I was having a heart attack.

My mother's face flashed by. I wanted to shout for her, but my lungs had quit for good, my tongue a rigid piece of meat. She'd find me in the morning dead on the carpet. My sight turned foggy then black. I was passing out. I sucked frantically and drew in a bit of air. Slowly with each breath the crushing heaviness subsided.

Blinking away the haze, I wiped my sweaty forehead. I should make an appointment with the family doctor.

Something moved ahead. There at the edge of a clearing cowered the man in rags holding his right elbow. He trembled and now that I was closer, I saw blood dripping from his wrist. The three riders had surrounded him, their blades pointing toward the man's neck. One rider dismounted, his face shadowed by a half helmet and curled brownish beard, his hands covered by steel gauntlets like lizard scales. The other two sat motionless, waiting. I tried to get a better view of what the horsemen were doing when I looked down.

And froze.

I stood on the gnarled root of an oak tree. Surely I imagined things. But those were definitely *my* Nikes I'd forgotten to take off when I returned home. I moved my foot. Leaves crackled. A twig snapped. Something terrible had happened, something I couldn't wrap my mind around. I blinked and looked to my right. Trees and undergrowth were losing themselves in the gloom. I remembered the mouse in my right hand, but when I lifted my arm, my fingers came up empty—except for the smear of something sticky on my palm. Blood. I was *bleeding.*

Wait.

The bush next to me was covered in blood. Not mine, I realized with relief. Disgusted I wiped my shaking hands with a fistful of leaves and turned to look behind me. The woods stretched into darkness—shadows within shadows nearly black.

My room was gone.

CHAPTER TWO

I heard more rustling. Louder now. Not from the men, but from the woods behind me. My knees buckled and I was vaguely aware of the thudding sound I'd made. I had to figure out what had just happened, retrace my steps. *Where was my room?* My mind churned as I scanned the ground for some sign of home, something familiar.

Out of the corner of my eye I saw the bearded thug turn his head. Ducking behind a hazelnut bush, I squinted through the leaves. The thug had raised his sword and stepped toward my hiding place.

I crouched lower, my ears filled with the pounding of my own heartbeat. Rough laughter came from the other two riders. Despite my panic I caught a glimpse of them poking their swords at the injured man's shoulder. I smelled their stench—and the wounded man's fear.

The bearded thug continued in my direction. Sunlight bounced off the edge of his blade. He took another step, scanning, listening. I forced my shaking body to be absolutely still. This had to be some kind of challenge in the game.

The man kept coming. Twenty feet. Everything about him looked menacing: his eyes the color of mud, his razor-sharp sword wide as a hand. Fifteen feet. I held my breath.

A scream rang out.

"Have mercy, My Lords," the bleeding man cried. He was kneeling now, waiving his good arm in a pleading gesture. "I beg you," he wailed.

I lowered my gaze. Somewhere I'd read that the white of a man's eyes could give one away. Keeping my lids half-closed, I peeked through the leaves once more. The thug was ten feet away. Close up he looked worse, a brute with arms the size of my thighs, his chest covered in leather and wide as a barrel. Despite his size he had the soundless walk of a stalking animal. I watched with paralyzed fascination. Any second I'd be discovered, but all I managed was to shove my hands into my jeans pockets to keep them from trembling. *It's a computer game*, my brain screamed. *It's real*, my gut argued.

"*Eilet Euch und bindet den Gefangenen.* We've squandered enough time." The rider spoke in some kind of medieval-sounding German, his voice icy and bored, but I was certain he'd said something like make haste and bind the prisoner.

The bearded thug hesitated. He glanced left and right and then abruptly turned. I gulped air, my ears ringing with waning adrenalin.

"I'll pay for the bread," the injured man cried. "I'll find..." the rest of his words turned to incoherent mumble.

The thug now towered over his prisoner, a giant ready to squash an annoying insect. The rider with the cold voice wriggled his sword in front of the man's nose.

"Teach him a lesson first."

"Let's cut off his hands." The bearded thug smacked his lips in anticipation as he lifted his sword above his head.

"No, please," the injured man cried. "I'll pay the Duke, I promise."

"Hold out your arms," the thug said, raising his sword higher. I blinked. I wanted to look away, but my eyes refused to move.

"The right middle finger," the rider with the icy voice said. "He won't use a bow again."

"Put your hand on the ground," the thug barked. "Or I'll cut it off and feed it to you." He sounded disappointed. The injured man leaned forward and stretched out his blood-covered hand.

That's when he saw me.

As the brute aimed the tip of his sword at the man's middle finger, the prisoner turned his head, our eyes meeting for the briefest moment. They were bluish-green like my own and filled with something like recognition. Had I imagined the man nodding? Before I could work out what I'd seen, I heard a soft crunch. A bloodcurdling scream rang out, the man's head whipping toward his mangled hand. He clutched his palm to apply pressure, his face drained of color. I finally looked away.

"Bind him," the rider said. He still sounded bored, but there was an element of urgency in his voice. "We shall leave before we run into Hanstein's guards."

The revolting stink of blood wafted across. I swallowed bile. I kept seeing the blood flowing from the man's palm, the empty spot where the middle finger had been. Do *NOT* puke. I began to tremble once more as the terror of being discovered turned my stomach. I was sure the prisoner had seen me. What if he told his captors?

I wiped my clammy hands on my jeans to distract myself. The guy had said Hanstein. The ruins of the old castle Hanstein were just up the street from my house. I'd seen them when my Uncle William visited from the States. Funny how much Americans loved medieval castles. Jimmy's dad had invented a game with his neighborhood castle? Not too creative if you asked me. *But how could this feel so real,* my mind whirled.

The back of my head stung as an acorn bounced to the ground, followed by a pinecone hitting my neck. I turned. Less than ten feet away, a boy about my age cowered in a pile of dried oak leaves. He had placed a rather grimy forefinger on his lips, his eyes wide with alarm and fury. I blinked again. Maybe this was all a dream and I'd simply fallen asleep while playing.

The boy gestured for me to come closer. While the thug dragged the prisoner to his feet and kicked leaves across the blood-soaked ground, I turned and crawled. Without a word the boy spun around and, head ducked low, ran into the shadows. I followed. My neck tingled as I imagined the soldier with the evil blade attacking from behind. Still, I never turned, afraid to stumble and crash. This *had* to be part of the game.

The boy was surprisingly fast and I had trouble keeping up.

At last, he stopped. "What're you doing in Hanstein's forest?" He waved a dismissive hand. "They'll slay us. You're not supposed to be here." The boy rolled the Rs, speaking fast.

I struggled to keep up. "What?"

"Are you daft, too?"

I stared at the filthy face. What was the guy talking about? Maybe it was best to start with the basics. "Who are you?" I said, digging deep to remember my German. Strangely, it came out easy.

"Bero. Who are you?"

"Max."

"What name is that?" Bero glared. "Are you thick or what, spying on the Duke's men?"

"What duke? What are you talking about, man?" I gaped at Bero who looked as if he hadn't combed his hair in a year and whose skin was crusted with filth. He was barefoot. The pants, with several holes and shredded at the bottom, barely reached past his knees. His shirt and neck were covered with more grime. A nasty odor surrounded him, attracting flies. They swarmed around his head, but he didn't seem to notice. I stepped backwards. Better to keep my distance in case the flies wanted another meal.

"Duke Schwarzburg's henchmen. They'll destroy us for watching them. So will the Lord."

"Who's Schwarzburg? What lord?"

Bero grunted in an obvious attempt to suppress an insult. "The Lords of Hanstein. They own these woods," he said slowly as if I were a moron.

Just as I formulated a snappy retort, the bushes behind Bero moved, followed by grunts and snorts. I stared in disbelief, a new wave of fear taking over my legs, my mouth too dry to speak. A dozen or so wild pigs with black, coarse bristles were rushing up to us.

Bero looked behind him and shrugged. "My sows…"

"Your pi…sows?" I stumbled. "Aren't they dangerous?"

Bero looked at me in disbelief. "*Ach*, you're chicken-hearted, too. And slow to boot." He clucked with disdain. "Everyone knows they're farm animals. I thought you were a brave lad, sneaking around the Duke's men."

If I hadn't been so confused I would've hurled back an insult. Domestic pigs were supposed to be pink. "What're *you* doing in the woods, if nobody is allowed?" I managed.

A slow grin spread across Bero's face. "Harvest is short and my sows got to eat. Woods have plenty of acorns, beech nuts and roots for all of us." He shrugged. "The Lords won't miss them."

"I see," I said, though I didn't, not really. "Where do you live?" I said to change the subject. Maybe I was supposed to ask questions so I could get the heck done with this stupid game. I wasn't playing to get jerked around by a stinking pig herder.

Bero pointed a thumb over his shoulder. "Yonder, the village."

"What village?"

"*Bornhagen*. You?"

"Same." It was out before I had time to think.

Bero stepped backwards, shaking his head in apparent alarm. His face, which had been full of scorn, turned to outright suspicion. "Nay, impossible. I'd *know* you." He slowly looked me up and down, his glance ending with my Nikes, shimmering white and silvery in the fading light. "You look nothing like us. Your robes are..." Bero seemed to have run out of words as he stared at my T-shirt and jeans. "Unless..."

"What?" I asked. "I'm playing the game." What was I saying? I was *in* the game and telling one of the invented figures of Jimmy's father that I was playing. *Duh*. "I mean I'm from nearby. I'm not sure."

Bero kept staring as if he were trying to make up his mind. "Nearby? Ha!" He spit into the leaves. "Nay, you look odd, your boots... Maybe you're working for Hanstein after all. A spy. You'll tell the Lord. They'll seize me and I won't ever be a squire."

"Squire?" I had trouble following Bero's rambling. It sounded like German, but then it didn't. More like a distant dialect. Even weirder, Bero seemed to understand me. That had to be the game.

With a sigh Bero slumped on the ground. His pigs had settled nearby, grunting and digging with long gray snouts.

"I'm no spy." I squatted next to the guy who all of a sudden looked forlorn. "I'm sort of...lost."

Still Bero said nothing while he pulled sticks and leaves from between his grimy toes.

"Would I stay with you if I were a spy? You know I was hiding just like you." I paused, thinking of the man's bloody hand. I shuddered and wondered if Bero had seen the whole thing. "Tell me about the squire stuff."

Bero shook his head. He glimpsed upward into the trees and sniffed. "It's eventide. *Mutter* will be mad if I'm late for supper. I'll get a whipping." He jumped to his feet, light and quick as a squirrel, letting out a low whistle at the same time. New grunts and squeaks erupted as the pigs assembled around their master. He squinted again in obvious distrust. "See you 'round...perchance."

To me it sounded like *leave me the heck alone*. I stood up, too. It was growing dark for sure. The shadows of the undergrowth looked inky and I could hardly make out the sky. Maybe this was a good time to take a break and search for a snack. Mom always had ice cream stashed in the freezer.

As Bero disappeared into the gloom, I turned 360 degrees. All I saw was dusk. All I heard was the song of some nauseatingly happy bird above me. I looked at my feet. I still stood in the woods and nowhere near on the carpet of my room. There was no pause button and no mouse.

I shivered. I was somehow *in* the game and clueless what I was supposed to do. All games had goals like winning points and completing missions, shooting demons or collecting gold. But every game had a pause button and you could exit any time. What in the heck was I supposed to do standing in the middle of a forest? I remembered the sickening sight of the man's bloody hand, the hole where his finger had been. Then there was the blood on my own hand. The foul smells. Never before, not even when my father had left, had I felt this alone...and scared. Games were supposed to be virtual *and* fun.

I wondered how much time had passed since I'd punched the *expert* button. It had to be hours. What if I didn't return by morning? My mother would freak out. I shook my head but nothing changed. Nothing except for new rustling to my right. It was much louder than the sounds of squirrels and birds. Who knew what dangerous animals Jimmy's father had dreamed up? Maybe he'd stuffed the forest with wolves and bears.

Renewed terror seized me. I stood absolutely still, forcing my brain into action. What if I were eaten by a bear? Was that even possible in a game?

Maybe I'd missed some hint. Jimmy would laugh at me in the morning. Okay, I'd skipped level one and gone straight to expert, obviously a huge mistake. Great gamer I was.

Struggling against the rising panic, I remembered Bero. Maybe if I could go with him until I'd find a clue and think things through. At least the guy knew his way around, even if he looked like he'd spent a year in the landfill. He didn't sound exactly stupid, despite the fact he talked weird.

Without another thought, I broke into a run in the general direction Bero had taken... which turned into a sprint, something I hadn't done since last year's track season. The twilight turned everything gray, but I noticed the faint signs of broken sticks and upturned leaves the pigs had left.

"Bero?" I yelled. I kept running, my lungs tight, thighs burning.

In the vanishing light at the edge of the forest, the land fell in a gentle slope toward…*what?*

Where the neat homes and hedged gardens, the paved roads and street lanterns of Bornhagen had been, shacks and huts squatted in the dusk, crooked and dirty with thatched roofs and muddy paths. This couldn't be right. I'd spent two years in Bornhagen. I knew every street and nearly every house. I had to be in some other place, maybe one of those make-believe medieval villages, some kind of tourist attraction.

Bero's slight figure scampered along two hundred yards ahead.

"Wait for me," I shouted again, breaking into another run. At last I saw Bero stop. His pigs snorted loudly, impatient to get back to their stall.

"Thanks, man," I panted as I drew near.

"What is it?" Bero frowned. "I'm late. Sows need water."

I swallowed against the dryness in my throat, a sure sign I was nervous. I thought of what to say, tell the guy some bullshit story about being mugged or losing my parents in a bloody car accident, but somehow it seemed unlikely that Bero would fall for it. I decided truth was best.

"Look, I need a place to stay. Just for tonight. I'm sort of lost. I'm not from here, not exactly. I'll try to explain, but I know you're late. I'm no spy even if I sound strange to you. Fact is you're my only hope. Otherwise, I'll…have no place to go." I opened my mouth, but nothing else seemed right to say.

Bero stared, his gaze lingering on my shoes. A minute passed. Whether it was my explanation or the underlying fear that had made my voice shake, Bero finally nodded.

"You can come. But you must help with the sows. And don't mouth off to *Mutter*." Bero punched me in the shoulder, but I didn't mind. I was strangely relieved.

"Thanks, man."

At the edge of the village a shack stood surrounded by a fence. Blackened timber crisscrossed its whitewashed and now gray outer walls, reminding me of a crooked chessboard. On the doorstep a girl of about twelve sat shelling beans by a smoldering light. She didn't look up until Bero opened the gate and shooed his pigs into an enclosure with a low-roofed barn. I slinked along.

"*Mutter* is cross with you," the girl shouted in Bero's direction. When her eyes fell on me, she began to stare, her mouth forming a perfect O. I nodded. She shrieked and disappeared inside the hut.

Ignoring her, Bero pointed toward a wooden bucket that hung on the fenced-in pen. "Water troughs need filling. You have to go three times. Sows are thirsty after the long day."

I grabbed the pail and looked for a faucet. Surely it had to be near the house.

"What are you doing? Make haste," Bero said.

"Looking for the faucet."

"What's a faucet?"

"For the water." We stared at each other as if we were both fools.

Finally Bero shrugged and pointed down the path. "The well is that way. Make haste, I'm starving."

I ran past more crooked huts until I saw a circular wall with a crude roof above. Remembering vaguely what I'd learned in history class, I circled around it. The wooden crank, splintered and silvery from age, was encased in rusted iron. I gave it a shove and breathed a sigh of relief when I heard the sound of trickling water in the depth. It was nearly dark now except for a low shine escaping from the open door of Bero's hut. In the distance, I saw other lights. They were so dim that they looked more like fireflies than lamps. Jimmy's father sure had done a good job with this place. It looked pretty authentic, wherever it was.

"You dawdle like a drunken snail," Bero said after my third trip, snatching the pail from my hand and returning it to the barn wall. "Let's eat."

I wiped my damp hands on my jeans and followed Bero into the hut.

End of Chapter Two

Made in United States
Troutdale, OR
04/05/2024

18971953R10056